P9-CFT-835

AS THE WARD TURNS

A NOVEL
BY

JONI HILTON

Copyright © 1991 by Joni Hilton
All rights reserved
Printed in the United States of America

Covenant Communications, Inc.
American Fork, Utah

As the Ward Turns
ISBN 1-57734-019-1
Library of Congress Catalog Card Number 91-73499

First Printing: October 1991
06 05 04 03 02 01 00 99   10 9 8 7

I dedicate this book to my husband, Bob, whose unofficial calling as Relief Society president's husband puts him in the Husband Hall of Fame.

A NOTE FROM THE AUTHOR

Serving as the Relief Society president of the Tarzana Ward, I've wondered more than once if my hilarious, trying, and amazing experiences could be because I'm serving in the only ward in the Church to name itself after a jungle man in a loincloth. But after extensive research (okay, a lot of chatty consultation) I've realized that these adventures are everywhere. So, while this book is not about my actual experiences—which would carry the unbelievable ring that true life always does—it is about the predicaments inevitably found when two or more are gathered. Except for a few of Andy's klutzy moves, and one or two comments from my children, all of the people and incidents in this book are fictional. I must admit, there's a relief all its own in knowing that.

CONTENTS

THE SHOO-IN

Edith Horvitz built her entire house using particle board and a hot glue gun. I couldn't think of a better qualification for homemaking director in all the Church.

Here we were, limping along with the lowest homemaking night attendance of any ward in the stake, when suddenly—as if the heavens had opened and plunked down our ringer—we heard of Edith Horvitz.

"Is this a miracle or what?" I asked my counselors. "She'll be getting the women to come out by the vanload! We'll have to divide the ward because of her incredible talents alone."

We were driving over to her house as a presidency to welcome her to the Relief Society board. "Why haven't other presidencies thought of her before?" I asked.

No one knew, and no one cared. All that mattered now was that we had her. She was our coup, our victory, our crafts queen who would take us galloping into the record books on a *papier-mâché* stallion. This was going to make history.

I pulled onto Clover Boulevard. Clovers . . . shamrocks—the symbols of luck, right? Here we were, driving right down the symbol of phenomenal fortune. I had always wanted to live in an allegory, and here I was.

My second counselor, Monica Baldwin, had scheduled our visit. I could just picture Edith Horvitz (though I'd never met her) happily awaiting our arrival. No doubt her eager brain would be packed with brilliant ideas, including both crafts and lectures that would appeal to young and old alike. Oh, Edith, I thought, we love you already!

"I can't believe she accepted such a big job when she doesn't even come out to church," Monica said. Monica is my homemaking counselor, my right arm, and the woman who got the trim little body I signed up for in the preexistence. "But she sounded really excited on the phone."

"It just goes to show you," Lara Westin, the first counselor, said. "When you let people know they're needed, they can't wait to come back." Lara is cheerfulness personified. On a women's retreat last year, a storm was howling outside our cabin and Lara actually started humming to it. She's encouraging, upbeat, and always sees the best in people. In other words, she's a freak of nature—but irresistible—and we all love her.

I turned off Clover onto Stable Street. "Hey, look—they must be making a movie," I said. Sure enough, there was a big mobile van, a catering truck, and a video remote trailer with lights, cables, and collapsible chairs strewn all over the road.

"Watch for the address," I said, creeping slowly toward the filming set.

"There it is!" Monica gasped, pointing to a hideous little house where the hub of the filming seemed to be.

"Look! Isn't that Phil Wallace?" Lara asked.

"Where?" Monica stared as I tried to pull over.

"There, in the blue blazer. Oh, I just love that show!" Lara was clearly on the brink of embarrassing all of us. I thought about automatically locking the doors. But the minute the van stopped, Lara had bolted out and was bounding across somebody's geraniums toward the man in mention.

"Who's Phil Wallace?" I asked.

Monica laughed. "Oh, come on, Andy, don't you ever watch that guy on the news who interviews all these weird people who turn out to be your neighbors?"

I shrugged. Never heard of it. But then, why should such a show surprise me? Local news seemed unaware of

escalating crime and world chaos. If they could do an
entire fluff segment on hamster clothes, such as I had
seen a couple of nights ago, then this "Neighbors" segment
must seem like "Meet the Press."

Monica had dashed from the car and was jogging over
to join the now gushing Lara.

Then I froze. Wait a minute. If that's one of those
shows about local yokels who turn out to be full-fledged
crackpots, and if the video unit is parked at Edith
Horvitz's house, that can only mean one thing—we had
made a serious mistake.

I slumped over the steering wheel. No wonder the
bishop had seemed so surprised when I asked him to call
Edith Horvitz to be our homemaking director. I should
have picked up on his concern when he asked, "Are you
sure?" All I'd been able to think about was the conversation I'd overheard in the hall about Edith Horvitz
and the infamous glue gun, which was evidently going to
make headlines today. Two women had been remarking
about how amazing the project was, and I seized upon the
information like a desperate Relief Society president.
(Okay, I was and still *am* a desperate Relief Society
president.) Let's face it. We had tried to get nearly every
woman in the ward to be our homemaking director, but
they were either moving, pregnant, or wise to us. Mostly
wise to us.

It's not a gigantic job. Really. Huge, maybe, but not
impossible. And with a committee to help . . . Oh please, I
thought. How could this be happening? I should have
prayed about it before I submitted Edith's name. Oh, why
didn't I do it right? Why did I jump the glue gun? Edith
Horvitz, how could you do this to us?

I glanced up at the filming crew and cringed.
Through the ponytailed swarm of lighting guys I could see
Lara raving. Her hands were clasped in delight—or
prayer. Hopefully prayer. Maybe this whole thing would
become a bad dream. No, her eyes were open and her
cheeks were flushed. She was definitely raving to some
guy in a parka.

Monica was shaking hands with Phil Wallace who

was using his other hand to pull at a tight tie. Clearly, he saw Monica as just another adoring fan. I took a deep breath, double-checked the address, and walked over to Edith's house.

And there it was—a monument to eccentricity. Not only was it made of particle board, but the roof was covered with circles of corrugated tin. If you were making a gingerbread house and decided to use Ruffles potato chips for shingles, this is how your house would look— except for the walkway. The walkway was made entirely of bottle caps embedded in concrete. "Oh, this can't be happening," I muttered to myself. Surely there were zoning laws, or taste laws, or something to prevent this kind of disaster.

"You must be Alexandra Taylor." Suddenly, standing before me was a balding woman in maroon lipstick, blue eye shadow, and an orange housecoat. She looked like Don Rickles in a muumuu.

"Andy," I mumbled, and shook her hand. "Call me Andy."

"I'm Edith Horvitz. Your hair's curlier than I expected."

"It's curlier than I expected, too," I said. "You know how it is when you get a new permanent—" I stopped. Of course she wouldn't know how it is. She didn't have enough hair to bother a comb, much less to perm. Well, now that I had put my foot in my mouth, we made a good pair—hairless Edith with that wild makeup and me with a head of frizzy hair and a foot in my mouth.

"I've seen electro-shock do that," said Edith. She was a very intense woman.

I sighed and smiled. No way was I going to touch that line. I wanted to welcome her to the board, to say how happy I was to meet her, anything. But instead I looked frantically for help. Where were Monica and Lara?

Just then a girl with horn-rimmed glasses and a clipboard came over and led Edith away for the interview.

"Hey, why do you think she had us come over when they're doing this story on her?" I turned. It was Monica, with Lara on her heels.

"Huh?" I felt like a zombie.

"Oh, now, cheer up. It isn't as bad as it looks," Lara said. "So the woman is a little . . . well, different. Sometimes you need a little spice to liven things up."

"Lara," I said. "This is not spice. This is an entire jalapeno pepper caught in the throat of the Relief Society."

"Now, now," Lara said, putting her arm around me.

Monica stared at the porch where Edith was standing. "Do you think anyone will ever come to home-making night again?"

"Thank you for giving us something pleasant to contemplate," I said.

"I think we'll get a great turnout!" Lara said brightly. Monica and I just stared at her. "You know," she went on, "the curiosity factor."

I closed my eyes. She was probably right. All the grumblers who typically stand on the sidelines and wait for the workers to burn out or goof up will be crowing over this one. They'll climb all over each other trying to get front row seats to watch us make lawn ornaments out of plastic twist-ties.

"Forgive me, you guys," I whispered. "I didn't pray about this one. I just—"

"Hey, it'll be fun," Monica said. "If nothing else, we can watch you writhe."

"You're a true friend," I said.

"Hey, Andy!" It was Edith, shouting from her front porch. "You and the other sisters come over here!"

Suddenly the film crew saw us in a new light. Before, we were just middle-class moms, a little starry-eyed around Phil What's-His-Name, getting in the way here and there. Now we were friends, maybe even relatives, of this extra-terrestrial glue woman. A camera turned on us.

"Oh, no," I hissed through smiling teeth.

"Come on," Lara whispered. "Maybe we'll get some publicity and that will counteract . . . you know."

Monica and Lara began strong-arming me toward Edith. I turned to Lara. "Have you gone completely bonkers? We need this kind of publicity like a hole—"

Suddenly there was a mike in my face, so I closed my mouth.

Phil Wallace said, "Sisters, eh? Are you nuns?"

I smiled. "Oh, we're thinking about it."

Lara nudged me and giggled. "No. We're members of the Church of Jesus Christ of Latter-day Saints."

Oh good, Lara, I thought. That ought to kill any possibility of missionary success for a few months. One look at this show and every viewer is going to size us up as a bunch of lunatics. Maybe a convent will be the only place where we can show our faces after all.

We stepped onto the particle board porch.

"I'm the new homemaking director at our church," Edith said, "requested by Alexandra Taylor."

Oh, please, don't use my name!

Edith's eyes narrowed into slits. "Specifically."

I gulped, and we all went into Edith's house.

Lara gave out a loud whistle and Monica nearly fainted.

"Come on, you two," I whispered. "Let's try not to overreact." And then I looked around and gasped. The entire living room, including the fish tank, was covered with multi-color crochet.

"Well, this is certainly amazing," boomed Phil.

Oh, Phil, put a lid on it, I almost said aloud. Leave this poor deranged woman alone and let us get on with the doomed year that lies ahead. Let us try to promote our homemaking nights all to no avail. Let us become the laughing stock of the stake. Let us fill our homes with crocheted televisions and crocheted mantels.

"This is Buster," Edith said, picking up a crocheted poodle. "You can pet him. He won't bite."

No kidding.

"Well, how do you like that!" Phil was clearly as speechless as we were.

"I had a cat to go with him, but I think it ran away."

I laughed, then stopped quickly as I realized that Edith was serious. Monica gave me a look.

Edith kept talking to Phil. "These ladies want to explain my new job to me. You're welcome to listen in."

And then before we could politely reschedule, Phil (who sensed this could get even more insane) answered,

"That sounds just terrific! You all go right ahead."

"We can come back later, Edith," I said. "We didn't know you'd be busy—"

"Are you kidding?" Edith sounded angry. "I planned it this way on purpose, so they could see a typical day."

Of course she did. I smiled. "Well!"

The cameras were still rolling as Monica fell off the crocheted stool she tried to sit on. It turned out that the stool was one of those inflatable jobs. But covered with crochet, who would know? Then, I got my high heel stuck in the crocheted rug we were standing on, and as I stepped toward the sofa to sit down, the rug pulled my shoe off. I remember thinking, "It's alive! We're under attack! This house is going to devour us." I could imagine the Movie of the Week they'd make about it: *Venus House Trap*, or maybe, *Stable Street: Misnomer of the Century*.

Lara tried to sit down on a chair, but jumped up with a scream, rubbing her backside. When Edith marched over to investigate, she happily announced the discovery of her lost knitting needles. And then the *coup de grace*: Lara actually laughed and hugged her. All the while, Phil was eating it up.

"I'm telling you, it was like Goldilocks in triplicate," I told Brian, my husband, that evening. "Everything we sat on either unraveled or exploded. And that creepy Phil Wallace just lapped it up. We'll be the laughing stocks of the whole community and Phil Wallace will win an Emmy Award."

Brian was straining neck muscles trying not to laugh. He kept munching on celery to occupy his mouth while I made dinner. "Don't you laugh about this, Brian Taylor," I said. "This will not be funny for five years, at least."

Brian's eyes grew wide and innocent. "I wasn't going to laugh." His voice was squeaking.

"Seriously. It was like Grimms' Fairy Tales—with emphasis on Grimm. Before the Goldilocks thing, it was just like the 'Three Little Pigs.'" I put the garlic bread into the broiler.

Brian smiled. "I can smile, right? Smiling is okay?"

"Picture it," I said. "The three little pigs had this one other brother, okay? The fourth little pig. But we never hear about him, because nobody would believe it."

"I see. Whereas we *do* buy the other pigs' stories."

"Hey. Anybody could think of building a house from sticks or straw or bricks. Brian, . . ." I glanced into the family room, where the kids were engrossed in homework and piano practice. Then I lowered my voice. "Nobody in their right mind thinks of particle board and hot glue."

"You did. You thought it sounded ingenious. Isn't that why you picked her?"

I wish I could describe the emotional pain you feel when you realize that you have more in common with the ward madwoman than you do with the former Relief Society presidents, all of whom were wise enough not to make your mistake.

Brian, seeing my weakened position and anguished brow, seized the opportunity to laugh. He didn't just chuckle, he laughed high squealing gales that brought tears to his eyes and pain to his sides.

"I'm so glad that I can contribute to your home entertainment," I said. "I know you've certainly added to mine."

Brian was wiping his eyes on a napkin and coughing.

"Oh, choking on the celery, dear?" I asked. "Let me call for help. Let's see. What was that number? Hmm . . . oh well, it will come to me." I got the plates out of the cabinet and set them on the counter.

"Erica, your turn to set the table," I called. Instantly the piano drills ceased and our ten-year-old daughter appeared. She scooped up the plates and whizzed into the dining room.

Brian took me in his arms, gazed romantically into my eyes and said, "I can't wait until the news comes on." Then he burst into more laughter.

I grabbed a dish towel and swatted his head with it. "You know, you have almost as much hair as Edith," I said.

"You're kidding. She's bald?" Brian's hairline had started receding in college and was now but a shadow of its former self. "Hey," he said, "maybe you could lend her some of yours, now that you have . . . you know . . . so much and all."

Brian knew I was furious about my permanent-gone-wild. He giggled with self-satisfaction over his well-delivered jab.

"I *wanted* it to look this way," I said. "Because you have to look at it and I don't!" In truth, I looked like those pictures you see in the encyclopedia of people who are demonstrating how static electricity can make your hair stand on end. Only their hair stands out straight; mine stood in frizzy little coils.

"You know, the great thing about that hairdo," Brian went on, "is that even when you're tired, you look full of electri—I mean, energy."

"Come on, Brian, stop teasing," I said. "I need help."

"I know you do, honey." He patted my hair. "And we're going to get you the best doctors . . . the *best!*"

I pushed him away, laughing and furious all at once.

"Andy, the time to ask for help was when you were supposed to be praying about who to request. Now you're getting some of those famous consequences you're always telling the kids about."

I sighed. "So what do I do?"

At last, Brian either ran out of material or took pity on me and turned serious. "You'll do fine. Monica is a great worker and she'll pick up the slack."

"But she doesn't *want* the slack. It's not her job."

"You have a whole homemaking committee. And anyway, Edith may surprise you."

"She has *already* surprised me." I lifted the pork roast out of the oven, then glanced into the family room, where our two boys were tumbling over the coffee table. "Isn't it bedtime yet?"

Brian hugged me again. "Look at the bright side. You've wanted to reactivate some of the sisters, right? Well, look at you. No one else has been able to get Sister Horvitz to take a job, and now you've gotten her involved."

"Brian," I said. "No one before has *offered* her a job— Edith is reactivated the way a deadly robot is reactivated.

She's suddenly alive again, storming the metropolis."

"I thought you really wanted every sister to come out to church."

"Oh, I do—even Edith. But Edith told us she only wants to plan our homemaking nights. She has no intention of coming out. So now, instead of getting more women active and eventually to the temple, we're going in the wrong direction. We're going to be losing them by the dozen."

"Why won't she come out to church?"

"She says she has to stay home to guard her collection."

"What collection?"

"Crocheted dogs. Don't ask. The point is, we're going to have the weirdest homemaking nights in history, and it won't even be worth it because we won't get her to come out to church after all." I poured some glazed carrots into a bowl.

"She sounds pretty eccentric." Brian and I carried food into the dining room.

"Eccentric?!" I whispered. "Your Uncle Pete living on a sailboat is eccentric. This is . . . I don't know what."

"You think she's really crazy?"

I sighed. "Well, when the time comes for preboarding on the jet to the celestial kingdom, I think the clearly-unaccountable Sister Horvitz is a shoo-in."

Brian laughed. "You're probably right."

"Meanwhile, unless I can learn to tolerate and embrace all these . . . these turquoise poodles of hers . . . I'm stuck on standby."

Brian smiled and rubbed my shoulders. "You're a pretty smart cookie, you know that?"

I pouted. "Yeah . . . smart enough to know that I've got to find a way to work with Edith Horvitz, or else. The catch is having to forgive people and endure valiantly and all—"

"And suffer the consequences of our actions . . ." Brian touched his nose to mine, still smiling.

"Yes. It all sort of—"

"Cramps your style a little bit, huh, Andy?"

I tried to glare at the man who can always see right

through me, but laughed instead. "Yes. It certainly does. Brian, she may as well have had a big neon sign on the roof that says, 'Andy, this is your test.' I knew the minute we got there."

Brian lit the candles. "You'll do fine."

We called the kids to wash their hands and went back into the kitchen.

"How did Phil Wallace hear about her?" Brian asked.

"Who knows?" I muttered. "Evidently insanity plus inactivity equals stardom."

"Whereas, if you keep your senses about you and stay active in the church, you will die an unknown," Brian said in mock solemnity.

"That's pretty much the lesson of the day," I said.

"Do you really think this is going to make home-making night all that disastrous?"

"Hey, we're poised on the brink of disaster as it is. And now this!" I grabbed some serving spoons. "Is it wrong to want things to be successful?"

"It can be. Sometimes you have to step back and let people do things their own way, good or bad. Maybe everyone will learn some tolerance—and humor."

"Maybe she'll ask to be released," I said, and then I remembered that Edith had said she had at least ten years' worth of ideas for us.

"I think she sounds kind of interesting," Brian said. "Did you think to ask her why she chose particle board over some of the other laminates?"

I just stared at him.

He laughed, then pulled me close to whisper. "Did I ever tell you what great legs you have?"

I started laughing. "Oh no you don't. You're just trying to . . . cheer me up or something."

Brian pretended to be ashamed. "I know it's terrible. I'm trying to quit."

I hugged him for a moment and thought. "Thanks. You always remind me of the important things in life," I said.

"Legs."

"I meant laughter. Anyway, thanks."

We kissed and Brian whispered into my ear, "Hey. As

long as we have one of the top ten great temple marriages in the world, what else matters?"

"Yu-u-u-u-ck!" Ryan, our five-year-old, came around the corner just as Brian and I were kissing.

"Sorry, son," Brian said, winking. "Didn't mean to gross you out."

Ryan walked out again, twirling one finger and pointing to his head.

"At least the kids will be in bed when the news comes on tonight," I said.

"See?" Brian smiled. "You're looking on the bright side already. Let's eat."

CURLY, MOE, AND LARRY—PRESIDING

You know you're in trouble when the bright side you're looking on is the fact that your kids will be asleep when you humiliate yourself on prime-time television. You know you're in *major* trouble when every one of your kids' friends has parents who will watch and then call to hee-haw over it and who—you know without a doubt—will tell their kids, who will then tell your own kids. That is exactly what happened.

Brian and I had just gotten Ryan, the night owl, to nod off in his bed, when the news came on. I stared with anticipation at the screen, waiting for the inevitable. Soon we heard an announcer boom, "Next up, Phil Wallace with 'NEIGHBORS!'" Suddenly the screen was filled with a close-up of Edith's face.

"Great Scott!" Brian shouted.

"Shh! You'll wake the kids."

"Is that her?!" Brian, to put it mildly, was stunned. "She wears black lipstick?"

"Maroon. I guess it looks black on TV."

"She looks like Grandpa on the Munsters, except without as much hair."

"Shh. Listen."

"Is this woman *your* neighbor?" Phil was asking. The camera cut to a grinning Phil. "Well, this time, you'd know if she were, because this house would be in your neighborhood."

And there it was, Edith's house in all its glory. "It

looks like graham crackers and potato chips," Brian whispered.

Phil went on to describe how Edith had made the thing. Then he said, "We happened by the same day as some women from Edith's church."

"'Happened by,'" I said to Brian. "Right." Suddenly, there we were on the porch, looking like we were lined up for execution. Phil went on, "Looks like these women were equally impressed with Edith's talents."

"Alexandra Taylor. Specifically." Edith looked as if she were reading off a hit list.

Brian winced. His wife had been publicly identified.

Slowly the camera panned our smiling faces. Every one of us looked too stupid to realize we were being had. In quick edits, there were shots of Monica falling off the stool, me losing my shoe, and Lara popping up off the knitting needles.

Brian snickered. "I'm sorry, honey. But you've gotta admit, it's pretty . . ." He cleared his throat and tried to be serious again. ". . . terrible."

"We're dead," I whispered.

"Edith lives in a virtual museum," Phil was saying, as the camera panned her endless crochet work. Then Phil was saying to Edith, "This is quite a collection, Edith. I'm sure you keep it well-protected."

Edith's eyes lit up. "You think I should? You think it could really be worth something?"

"Oh, absolutely." Phil was lying worse than a crocheted rug.

Edith's eyes narrowed again. "Good idea. You can't let a collection like this go unguarded."

I let out a furious growl. "So this stupid show is the reason Edith won't come to church now! Thanks a lot, Phil!"

"Look! A rifle case!" Brian was mesmerized. And sure enough, there was a close-up of a yellow crocheted rifle case. "Hey, maybe she'll do a homemaking night on target practice. You could have Sharpshooter of the Month instead of Sister of the Month." Brian grinned.

"I married a genius."

"Hey, there's the famous glue gun." Evidently Brian felt compelled to give a play-by-play commentary.

I stared at the screen and imagined Edith holding us all hostage in the cultural hall, armed only with her glue gun and crochet hooks.

Now the camera was back on our presidency, sitting precariously on assorted chairs in Edith's living room. We could be seen talking although the only audio was a narration by Phil. But the video had been cleverly edited so that just when Lara asked Edith how long she had been hooking rugs Edith could be heard to say, "Oh, I've been a hooker for most of my life."

And then, as if that weren't outrageous enough, we heard Lara's enthusiastic response, "Oh, you have such amazing talents!"

Next they showed us all bidding Edith a cheery good-bye. Then Phil went up to her and asked the name of her church again. "I'm a Mormon," Edith said.

"Uh-oh," Brian said. "You don't suppose the Church will sue you guys, do you?"

That's when the segment ended and the phone rang.

"You answer it," I said. "Use a foreign accent and say they have the wrong number."

"You don't even know who it is." Brian answered the phone, then whispered, "It's the bishop."

I knew it. "Hello, Bishop," I croaked.

"Well," he chortled, "I've seen some pretty imaginative schemes to get released in my time . . ."

I groaned. "Oh, Bishop, I feel so terrible about this. Are you upset?"

"Well, I'm not pleased. But it's the program I'm mad at. You I just feel sorry for. You didn't know about Edith, did you?"

"Obviously not."

"I thought that everyone knew about her being in and out of mental hospitals. That's why I was so surprised when you requested her. But I figured . . . maybe you were a friend of hers or something."

"Well, I guess I will be now."

Bishop Carlson laughed. "She'll keep you hopping."

"Yes, it looks that way."

"I'm going to call the producer of that show. The way they took things out of context . . . really low class."

"You think they can do anything about it? Maybe apologize or something?"

"We'll try. In the meantime, just don't answer the phone." Then he laughed again, more loudly this time.

"You're such a comfort," I said.

"C'mon, you're tough. You can take it."

"Well," I said, "if anyone asks you about it, just say I have an evil twin who's trying to wreck my reputation."

"What do you mean *your* reputation? I'm worried about the reputation of the Church! Boy, after that interview . . ."

I knew he was giving me a bad time now. "Yeah, you and Brian are having a field day with this. So do you think anyone will come out to church anymore?"

"Not after that!"

"Well," I said, "I had to do my part for the Lose My Sheep program."

Bishop Carlson laughed again. "You know what? I'll bet we get a surge in attendance. Seriously—everyone will come out to see you, Mo, and Lara now." He always teases Monica by calling her Mo. Then he hit upon his best idea for our presidency, the names he would call us forever more. "Hey, with that new curly hairdo, you guys can call yourselves Curly, Moe, and Larry. Get it? Lara—Larry?" He then began to hum the "Three Blind Mice" tune that has since become my nemesis. I held the phone out for Brian to hear, and whispered, "He wants to call us Curly, Moe, and Larry now." I sighed. "Well, I guess I'd better go. I have to book my reservations for Siberia."

He was still cracking up when I hung up. "A bishop with a sense of humor can be a good thing," I said to Brian. "But on the other hand . . . " The phone rang again. This time it was Monica.

"I have never been so humiliated in my life," she moaned. "How could this have happened to us? My mom wants to move out of the state. What will people think of us? It's terrible! Well, at least things can't get worse."

"Thanks, Monica. You always know just what to say."

The next call was Sister Delaney, who had once used a dead cat as a visual aid for a spiritual living lesson.

"Andy, I simply must express my feelings to you." Her voice began to crack and she seemed to be crying. "I have never seen anyone do more damage to this church than you and your counselors. I hope you have the courage to publicly apologize at church this Sunday. That's all I have to say."

"Sister Delaney, wait—" She had already hung up. "I can't believe that," I started to tell Brian, but the phone rang again.

This time it was Edith herself. "Pretty good missionary work, eh?"

I sputtered. "What?"

"It isn't every day you get the Church mentioned on T.V."

"No, that's for sure."

"Twice. How about that?" Edith was self-satisfaction personified. I closed my eyes. "Yes, it was twice all right."

"Maybe we can get 'em to cover the first homemaking night I do."

"Oh, I don't know, Edith . . ."

"Well, gotta go lock up. My house is on the map, you know."

The next four calls were all parents of our children's friends. Between howls of laughter they expressed 1) amazement that I would actually allow myself to appear on T.V. with my new permanent, 2) amazement that our church heralds people who glue their houses together, 3) amazement that their own problems now look so insignificant, and 4) amazement that we don't have our house up for sale.

"Is everyone we know a television addict?" I asked Brian. "Don't any of our friends ever read books or play Scrabble?"

Then Lara called. "Boy, has your line been busy!"

"I wonder why."

"I just thought I'd call to cheer you up. I thought we looked like good sports, didn't you?"

"Bless your heart, Lara, we did." For the first time all night, I smiled. "You just said the one thing that might pull me through this travesty. We were wonderfully good sports."

"I know you're worried about the missionaries having a hard time after this, but maybe it will be the opposite. Maybe now they'll have something to talk about."

"No doubt."

"Just imagine. People will want to ask about the show now. It will give the elders a chance to tell about home-making night, or how *everyone* is welcome in this church, or . . . to tell people what good sports we are."

"You're terrific, Lara. I don't know how I'd make it without you."

"That's what I'm here for."

"So you're not embarrassed and your husband isn't giving you a hard time?" I kicked my toe against Brian's shoe.

"Oh, Jerry thinks it's a kick." Jerry thinks everything is a kick. He and Lara are perfectly matched. I thanked her again and hung up.

"If we were pioneers," I said to Brian, "I'd want to be in Lara's wagon."

"But you're not. You're in Edith's wagon. And it's glued together."

I stared at him. "You still think this is funny."

"Hilarious."

With that, I pounced on him, rolled him to the ground, pulled his sweater, and began pummeling him. Through it all he kept giggling. "And you wonder why the kids roughhouse," he wheezed. "What an example. Oof!"

"You are a brat," I growled. "Sister Delaney said I should apologize Sunday."

Brian pulled one arm away. "Isn't she the one with the dead cat?"

"The only dead cat in the world who lives on in infamy," I said, and stomped off to bed.

Brian followed, still snickering as I took off my makeup.

"Does she really expect you to apologize?"

"Well, I'm not doing it. I'm the victim here, not the villain." I stood at the sink, soaping my cheeks.

"That's right."

"I mean, who does she think she is? How long does it take to develop that kind of empathy—a minute and a half?"

"That's right."

"She should be pitying me, not attacking me." I splashed warm water on my face.

"That's right. Tell her you'll apologize over her cat's dead body."

I laughed, inhaled some water, and began coughing at the same time.

"Do you need to throw up?"

"Oh, Brian, stop it! Get me a towel."

Soon we were giggling under the covers, planning all kinds of ridiculous statements to make on Sunday, none of which I would actually use.

Finally, we grew tired and Brian held me close. For the first time all evening, he grew serious. "This, too, shall pass," he said.

And it did. But not before my phone rang off the hook, the kids endured constant teasing at school, and Phil Wallace added a cheery, "Sorry to all the Mormons about the show last night," as he went on to highlight some woman in Sylmar who thinks she sees the Three Wise Men in a knothole in her trailer.

MISSION IMPOSSIBLE

Someday archaeologists will uncover ancient Mormon ruins and come to know everything about us from our wall plaques. Lara, who knows that you can indeed be too rich and too thin, has successfully avoided both predicaments. Over her stove a sign reads, "Life is Uncertain: Eat Dessert First." She has another over her breakfast bar, which says, "The Way to a Woman's Heart Is Through the Door of a Good Restaurant."

Monica's mother needlepoints almost as much as Edith Horvitz crochets, and thus Monica's walls ring with one wise adage after another. Most of them are thinly disguised reminders to Monica's wealthy husband that money isn't everything. One says, "The best things in life . . . aren't things." Another reads, "The golden age only comes to men when they have forgotten gold." Art, Monica's husband, finds his mother-in-law amusing and often quips that Evelyn is still trying to save Monica from marrying him and living in decadent misery.

Our secretary, Phoebe Burnfield, has "Love is a Verb" on her refrigerator right beside "When Mama ain't happy, ain't nobody happy."

However, as a group we're not hopelessly frivolous. Last year we had a series of calligraphy lessons on homemaking night, and now many of us also display some beautiful pictures of Christ, the prophets, and our temples, with quotes and scriptures carefully penned below.

But one of my favorite plaques is a tribute to my

grandfather, Erastus Samuels. He was the family philosopher—the least educated of any of the relatives, yet smarter than all the rest of us put together. He was outspoken and feisty, a no-nonsense farmer with a keen appreciation for hard work. But he knew exactly when to put that work aside if one of the grandkids needed him, and every one of us thought we were his favorite.

The quote over my desk is something he said to my grandmother the one summer when I visited them during my junior high years. I remember she was compassionate service leader at the time, and was asked repeatedly to drive one sister all over town. Every day it seemed she was off running Sister Beuman to the supermarket, the hairdresser, or the doctor.

One night for family home evening, Grandma read us the story of the fisherman who kept taking fish to his neighbor, then finally taught the fellow how to fish for himself. The ending goes, "Give a man a fish; you feed him for a day. Teach a man to fish; you feed him for a lifetime."

We all listened attentively. Grandpa leaned in, winked at Grandma, and said, "I got my own version of that story. It goes, 'Drive Ethel Beuman to the doctor and you drive her for the day. Make Ethel Beuman get a license and drive her own dang car and you buy the kind of freedom people fight wars for.'" Then he grinned. We all looked at Grandma, who was fuming but trying to maintain what she used to call "propriety." She took a deep breath, set her jaw, and said, "Thank you for that comment, Grandpa."

My cousins and I sensed a chill in the air, so we offered to get the refreshments in the kitchen. But I peeped out and saw the denouement: Grandma was slapping the living life out of Grandpa's arm, when suddenly he swept her into a big bear hug, kissed her right on the lips (not something we kids saw every day) and whispered to her. I saw her melt right there in his arms, smiling and nodding back at him.

The next day, Grandma drove Ethel Beuman to the Department of Motor Vehicles. After that, she never drove Ethel anywhere again.

I'd written down Grandpa's version of the fisherman story, and every time I see it I'm reminded that independence is sacred (and we must not rob others of it, even through our well-meaning favors). I also think of the lesson I learned watching Grandma listen to Grandpa. She rightly appreciated his sincere desire to see more of his wife!

Sometimes, through trying to do a good job as Relief Society president, I've found myself "driving Ethel Beuman" too much. At those times Brian has whispered, "Ethel Beuman?" to let me know he'd like his wife back. And it's helped. This job could easily consume every waking minute, and if I'm not careful, it could consume my family too. When first called to be Relief Society president, it took me awhile to recover from the awesome realization that I was now mother to the 180 women in our ward (as well as all the non-member women within our ward boundaries). I prayed about how I could meet all their needs. I really wanted to get around to visit every less-active sister in the ward, not just the ones who need us on occasion because they're sick, lonely, or recently home from the hospital. It was an overwhelming task. When I added up the hours that the various meetings took each month, I knew something had to give.

That's when I came up with "car meetings." I determined we'd have presidency meetings and visiting teaching meetings as we drove along to visit the various sisters. There was plenty of time to go over business as we rode along, plus we got to see about a dozen sisters a month this way. When all four of us (including Phoebe, our secretary) came to visit, nearly everyone let us in. Several sisters were even reactivated once they realized that some of us truly cared about them.

It was during one such car meeting that we decided to target three specific sisters to reactivate.

"How about Jorja Willis?" Lara suggested.

This brought on gasps and chokes from Monica, who sounded as bad as my BMW (Big Mormon Wagon). "Are you kidding? Don't you remember why she stopped coming out?"

"Yes, but I think she needs to get on with her life."

"Maybe you're right," I said. I remembered hearing that the creative folks at Disney had one rule in a meeting: Never say no to any idea. That way, nobody feels inhibited by possible rejection and every idea gets thoroughly explored. (I'll admit I couldn't help wondering, though, how many Disney executives would agree with Lara if they knew Jorja's story.)

Monica's mouth was still hanging open. "That's the last person I would have picked." Monica would never make it working for Disney.

"Let's try it," I said. "What's that saying—'They said it couldn't be done, and so he went right to it, and tackled the thing that couldn't be done—'"

"And couldn't do it." Phoebe smiled. "That *is* how it goes, right?"

I sighed. "Not exactly."

"Why don't we pick someone who's at least *possible*?" Monica said.

Lara laughed. "Jorja may well be impossible, but that just means it will take a little longer—to paraphrase another saying."

Phoebe chuckled and Monica looked at me for some backup. I laughed. "I say we give it a try. You never know what can happen when the Holy Ghost touches someone's heart."

Defeated, Monica slumped back in her seat. "You're having delusions of us being the A-Team or something."

I thought about Jorja's story. Years ago, Jorja Willis had had a son. Her husband had chosen the name Leslie for him. Three years later Jorja discovered that her husband had named their son after a woman he was having an affair with. Furious, she divorced him. But her story doesn't end there. She moved into our ward and raised her son alone. David (her son's middle name) grew up, became a stock broker, married in the temple, and had three children. Then, one day, he ran off with Lorene, a secretary from the office. Jorja was mortified. She blamed the secretary entirely. And then the worst blow. David's wife moved back East with Jorja's grandchildren, and she wasn't allowed to see them anymore.

David and the secretary soon broke up, but not before his family was torn apart, along with Jorja's heart. Perhaps in hopes of starting anew, David began going by the name Leslie again. In addition to Jorja's fresh wounds, this opened up old wounds.

Three years later, the missionaries taught a young woman, who repented, was baptized and became a member of our ward. She was none other than Lorene, the woman Jorja felt had cost her her grandchildren. That was the day Jorja became inactive.

"Boy, you sure like a challenge," Brian said that night, as he dug into a slice of lemon pie.

I grinned. "Yep."

"You really think you're going to get her to come to church again with Lorene Hausman teaching Primary?"

"Yep."

Brian shook his head, then smiled. "Who else did you pick?"

"Zan Archer."

Brian laughed, thinking I was kidding. "Right."

"We did."

"No way."

"Yes way. Watch us."

"Ooh-hoo! Look out, Lucifer."

"That's right. Guess who else." I mashed pie crust crumbs into my fork.

Brian stared at the walls, thinking. "Claudia Lambert."

"How did you know?"

"Andy, come on. You can't be serious."

"Oh, we're absolutely serious. You don't think we can do it, do you?"

"You're feisty tonight. You just want somebody to say you'll never do it so you can prove them wrong. You're fueled by spite."

I laughed. "I am not. Well, a little, maybe."

"Why did you pick the three least likely women in the whole ward?"

"Well, it started with Lara. She picked Jorja. Then

Monica, since she couldn't talk Lara out of it, decided to go one better and picked Zan. You know, just to be really ridiculous. Then Claudia kind of fit into that same category or something. I don't know." The hopelessness of our task was starting to sink in. "I guess we wanted to pick the three toughest nuts to crack."

"Well, if it's nuts you need, these women certainly qualify."

I laughed. "They do not. Every one of them is sane . . . I think."

Brian laughed. "But look. You picked Jorja Willis, who will never forgive Lorene Hausman—and who can blame her? You've got Zan Gloria Steinem Archer, who's president of three corporations and wouldn't come to church on a bet. And then you picked Claudia Lambert, whose nose is still out of joint just because people said she was a sloppy housekeeper."

"Looks pretty bleak, huh?" My confidence was draining fast.

Brian smiled, suddenly proud. "Nah. If anybody can do it, you guys can. Just don't eat at Claudia Lambert's."

"Brian!"

He shrugged. "Am I wrong?"

"How do you know so much about Claudia Lambert, anyway?" I covered the pie and put it in the refrigerator. "I've heard she has never even answered the door for anyone."

"Oh—I heard a story that happened before we moved into the ward. It seems some guys in the elders quorum were helping Claudia's next-door neighbors move. While they were loading boxes into somebody's truck, one of the little kids in the family looked through Claudia's window and then shouted for help. Three of the men ran over and looked in too. They saw chairs tipped over and piles of things all over the place. They figured there had been a scuffle or a robbery or something so they called the police."

"Oh no!"

"Oh yes. So the squad cars pulled up, sirens blaring, guns pulled, and they banged on Claudia's door. She came to the door in a towel—I guess she'd been in the shower."

"Brian, you're making this up."

"I am not! Ask Brother Henderson. He was there. In fact, I think he's the one who called the police. Anyway, it turned out her house was just really messy. Needless to say, with three elders and assorted policemen staring her down, she was absolutely humiliated."

I shook my head. "The ironic priesthood to the rescue. Poor Claudia."

"Poor Sister Mills," Brian said. "She was the Relief Society president then. She heard about it and figured Claudia needed someone to lighten her load. So she got one of Claudia's kids to let her and about five other Relief Society sisters in one day, and they cleaned up Claudia's house."

"Well, that was nice of them."

Brian raised his eyebrows. "You think so? The way I heard it, Claudia loaded a rifle and told them if they or their PineSol ever set foot in her house again, there'd be a mass funeral in the stake center."

I gulped. I wondered if we could order bulletproof vests through the ward clerk.

Brian took my hand. "Hey, you're white as a sheet."

"Gee, I wonder why. Do we need to talk about what kind of woman you should marry if I happen to die early?"

Brian laughed. (Our last conversation on this matter ended with my insisting that if he ever remarried, the woman had better have a curly tail and thick, bristly hair on her back.)

"C'mon, Claudia won't be mad at a whole new presidency. She's had ten years to get over this." Brian rinsed off our dishes and put them in the dishwasher. "You coming to bed?"

"Yes. In a few minutes."

Brian headed up the stairs, and I glanced around the room. I picked up a jacket, straightened some newspapers, scooped toys into a chest, and stacked some books on a shelf.

Then, just to be on the safe side, I closed the curtains.

STORMS AND SHOWERS

I finally learned why Zan Archer has risen to the top of the business world despite being only thirty. I called her to ask if she would lecture on investments at homemaking night. But, after I introduced myself and before I could get another word out, she quickly thanked me for calling to see how she was feeling after her bout with the flu. She went on and on about how wonderful I was to take time from my busy day just to see if she was all right. "Most people call me to ask for favors," she said. "But here you are, just showing genuine concern. No wonder you're the Relief Society president."

Yeah. No wonder, I thought. "Well, I'm glad you're doing so much better," I said at last. Somehow, I thought to myself, I've got to learn how Zan does that.

I decided to wait a few days, then write her a note of invitation. You can't interrupt a letter, right?

But by coincidence, or maybe it was divine intervention, a week later I found myself sitting beside Zan at a bridal shower. Julie, one of Zan's many secretaries, was a girl I had taught in Young Women. She had invited both her boss and me to her shower. Zan swept into the party wearing a power suit, her hair in a perfect business coiffure. Dripping with gold and perfume, she settled into an armchair as if it were first class seating on a jetliner.

"Wow," I whispered, staring at the giant diamond ring on her hand. "Can you get HBO on that?"

Zan stared at me for a second, then threw her head

back and laughed. "I'm Zan Archer," she said, extending
her hand. "And you're . . . ?"

"Andy Taylor. I called you, and sent you an—"

"Yes! So you're the Relief Society president." She
beamed. "I got your note. I'm terribly sorry, but I'm just
too busy traveling to do lectures. But I thank you for
inviting me."

"How about a lecture on how to say no? You just did
that so well." We both laughed.

Then Zan winked. "Well, it's something you have to
learn when you're running an organization. Haven't you
found that?"

"Well . . ." I said, "Actually I'm hoping to find it. I do
keep looking." Zan laughed again.

Julie's maid of honor handed out pencils and paper.
"Memorize everything on this tray," she said, holding out a
cookie sheet laden with such marriage essentials as mas-
sage oil, bubble bath, movie tickets, a tiny cookbook,
candy hearts, dried flowers and numerous other goodies
you rarely see when you're actually married.

Then she covered the tray and darted into the
kitchen. "Now write down all you can remember," she
said. Without looking up, I remembered that Zan was
wearing three gleaming bracelets, a diamond pin in the
shape of a Z, a cream and tan silk tie, suede pumps, and
designer sunglasses looped over the strap of her matching
suede handbag. But somehow I didn't think this was what
the maid of honor had in mind.

Everybody scribbled quickly until a timer went off.
"Who remembered five items?" asked the maid of honor.
We all had. "Ten? Fifteen? Twenty?" Eventually the ranks
were thinned until I was pronounced the winner and
received a package of bath pearls as my prize.

"How did you remember so many?" Zan asked.

"Oh, I cram for these shower games," I said. "I was up
until two-thirty studying for this one."

Zan laughed. "Cramming for a bridal shower!"

"The truth is, my kids' bedroom floors all look like
that cookie tray. I know at a glance if they've picked up
any of the things I've told them to. An hour later, I can

say, 'And what about the sock in the corner,' and they'll run back upstairs to finish."

Zan gave me a playful nudge and glanced at my bath pearls. "And they say motherhood has no rewards."

I smiled. Soon Julie was opening bath towels and can openers like a pro. Everybody oohed and ahhed over the chafing dish from Monica and the crystal pitcher from Zan. These are always the gifts that precede mine. No matter how big the pile of gifts is, mine is sure to be opened after the granddaddy of them all.

Julie picked up my pocketknife-sized gift and turned it over in her hands.

"It's a cigarette lighter," I said.

"Honestly, Andy," she mumbled, tearing off the wrapping. "Hey—it really is a lighter."

Everyone in the room gasped.

"Just kidding," Julie said. I rolled my eyes.

She lifted the lid off the box, and carefully removed the gift. "Oh—it's a Christmas ornament! For our first Christmas! It's gorgeous. Oh, Andy!"

Lara's gift was next. She was beaming, so I knew trouble was brewing. Whenever Lara beams, look out. Julie pulled at the bow.

"Here, let me break the ribbon for you," Monica said.

"Swiss Army Nails," I whispered to Zan.

Finally Julie began lifting out the contents of Lara's package: A tape of romantic music, a bottle of exotic oil, a scented candle and a lace teddy.

"I call it Honeymoon Helper!" Lara squealed.

The room erupted into giggles and laughs. I looked at Zan. "Who is that woman?" Zan whispered.

"My first counselor," I said. "She's quite a character."

"I can tell," Zan said, smiling.

As we were all leaving, Zan shook my hand again. "Tell you what," she said. "If you don't mind working with my schedule, I'll do the lecture."

"What? You will?" I tried not to fall over. "Great!"

She smiled. "It's been a long time since anyone made me laugh. Thank you."

I gave her a hug and she drove off in a sleek black

Porsche. Lara walked up beside me. "She's going to do the lecture!" I whispered. We had all thought that might be a way to get her to come out. "I think it's because she laughed and had a good time tonight."

Lara clapped her hands. "I knew it! I knew that Honeymoon Helper was a whizbang idea!"

Whizbang?

"I should have called it homemaking night helper, huh?" Lara giggled all the way to her Honda.

The next morning I got three calls. The first was from one of Zan's secretaries, booking the lecture and asking for a letter of confirmation and a map to the church.

The second was a new sister in the ward, Justine Overland, asking for details about the church welfare farm. She wanted to know the date the fruit was scheduled to be picked and if I would I mail her a map.

The third call was from Marla Verdugo, a newlywed who had just moved into the ward. "Gary and I are splitting up," she said. "Will you help me pack?"

Once I determined that she meant business, I quickly stuffed the maps into their envelopes and mailed them on my way to the Verdugos' apartment. Marla was standing on the balcony in a bathrobe as I drove up. "Up here, Sister Taylor," she called.

I ran up the stairs, hoping I could help her see a way to salvage the marriage before she actually moved out. Instead, she gave me specific instructions on how to wrap the dishes in newspaper and how to load the boxes. It turned out that the dishes reminded her of her marriage commitment and she was too upset to deal with it. While I packed, Marla decided she should take a hot shower and get dressed.

It felt odd to stand there by myself, wrapping up a stranger's things. Did Gary know about this? Was this kitchenware only Marla's? Had they tried to save the marriage or was this a hasty decision based on one argument? I wished she would come out and talk about the decision she had made.

An hour and a half later, Marla emerged looking well-rested. It turned out she *was* rested. "Sorry to be so long," she said. "I fell asleep."

Fell asleep?! How can anyone fall asleep when their marriage is crumbling? I was speechless.

"I guess it's all been too much for me," Marla went on.

"I'll need to be leaving soon," I said. "But I really wish you'd let me talk with you about this. I'd hate to see you make a mistake."

She hugged me and showed me to the door. "It's okay. Believe me, just knowing you were here to pack has really helped."

"Well, I really don't take sides—"

"Oh, I know. I'll be all right. Thanks for everything." I walked down the steps with eight packed boxes to my credit and a gnawing feeling that Marla was entirely too confident about her future.

When I walked into the house, the message light was flashing on the answering machine. I pushed rewind and play.

"Hi, Andy. This is Edith. You'll never guess what I did."

Oh, no, I thought. You called Associated Press and now the wire service has picked up your story.

"I found some pot pourri for homemaking night. A great big sack for just a dollar. So I bought ten. I figure it will go even farther if I borrow your food processor to grind it up a little. Then we can glue it onto those styrofoam balls and have great Christmas ornaments."

There is no way, I thought, that I'm letting her grind up pot pourri in my food processor.

The message went on. "I also found the cutest little straitjackets in size 2-T. I won't tell you where I got 'em. I figure they'd be perfect for keeping those little rascals in line during Sacrament Meeting."

I smiled. Why do I like this idea?

"Then I'm setting up a quilt," she went on, "and I'm calling it the Guilt Quilt. Every time you tie a knot, you stop feeling guilty about something."

I laughed. What a riot. Most of us could finish four or five quilts before we ran out of guilt!

"I'm still looking for a craft that uses pink pistachio shells," she said.

Pink pistachio shells? I couldn't remember Monica saying anything about that.

"It's just an idea of mine," Edith said, "Because I have several big bags full of them."

Good grief! I chuckled as I erased the message and headed into the kitchen. There, on the fridge, was a note for me. "Mom, I came home for lunch and let Edith Horvitz borrow the food processor. She said it was for homemaking night. Love, Erica."

I closed my eyes. While I was carefully wrapping Waterford crystal so it wouldn't break, Edith was dumping pot pourri onto the whirring, and soon-to-be-broken, blades of my Cuisinart.

I dropped by Edith's on my way to another errand, and sure enough, she *had* bought big bags of pot pourri for the astonishing price of one dollar—astonishing, until you looked into the bags and realized that these were redwood bark rejects—big chunks of wood that had been sprinkled with scented oil so that they could be passed off as pot pourri. There wasn't a rose petal to be seen.

My processor was history. However, Edith quickly added (since Lara wasn't present to point out this obvious bright side), she did pulverize lots of the wood before the machine broke. She was pretty sure we had more than enough.

That night, Marla Verdugo called to gleefully report that wedded bliss was hers once again—she and Gary had re-conciled. "Oh, I'm so relieved," I said. "That is just wonderful."

"Anytime you'd like to help us unpack, we'd really appre-ciate it," she said. "You packed so much we're amazed at how much work there is to do."

I sputtered. "Marla, I really don't know what to say. Why don't you get started. I think you'll find it will be done before you know it."

Silence. "Oh." More silence. "Well, we were going to go out and celebrate, but I guess we can stay home and *work*."

I took a deep breath and wondered what Zan would do. I could picture Marla's entire childhood. "I'll bet the two of you can make it very romantic," I said. "Bye, now.

And thanks again for the happy news."

That month at homemaking night, women made noisy maracas out of orange juice cans and pink pistachio shells. "If they don't scare off gophers, they'll help you train your dog," Edith said.

They tied a huge quilt and giggled over the silly things they felt guilty about. They hopelessly tried to glue hunks of wood onto styrofoam balls and found that while wood does not stick particularly well to styrofoam, it adheres incredibly well to wooden floors.

But best of all, they laughed themselves silly hand painting little straitjackets for their children. Grandmothers, aunts, and sisters couldn't wait to give the uproarious gag gifts to their relatives. Just the thought of "controlled" children brought a smile to their faces. Edith turned our homemaking nights upside down. We discovered that, just maybe, that's the way they should have been all along.

CHAPTER 5

CHICKS AT CHURCH

Here is what happens when the bishop goes out of town. First, there's a funeral. Next, three or four people have major surgery, all of whom have children with chicken pox who need babysitting. Then, pregnant women who aren't due for two months start having their babies. Husbands of these women are invariably unable to boil water, and must have all meals brought in until a grandmother arrives.

In addition to this, other wards ask to borrow your tables and chairs. Members who thought they'd borrow them for their daughters' garden receptions that same day feel enormously slighted. Members with nothing better to do begin taking sides on every ward issue imaginable and they all call the stake president, who, they assume, also has nothing better to do.

Then the church air conditioning system konks out, somebody misplaces all the hymn books, and four people get offended when someone gives a talk about exemplary ward members and doesn't mention them. In every case, the Relief Society mobilizes a task force to smooth feathers, deliver meals, get medicine, watch children, give hugs, mediate misunderstandings, and teach the gospel to wavering hearts.

All this we can handle. In fact, the core of hard workers in every ward mobilize like minutemen when these things happen. They've learned that the real secret to happiness is service. If you didn't ask them to help, they'd volunteer anyhow. But what I was utterly unprepared for, which, of course, happened when the bishop was out of town, was Lara Westin's talk show format fireside.

Months before, the bishopric had asked us to plan a fireside about Relief Society that the whole family would enjoy. No problem, I thought. Get a little choral group together to sing something terrific about being women. (How come men never sing about how great it is to be guys?) Then we could have some talks about our great pioneer foremothers or the role of women today— whatever the counselors wanted.

When I mentioned this assignment in presidency meeting Lara nearly had kittens. "Oh, let me plan it," she begged. "I have the best idea!"

Thinking how pleasant it would be not to be in charge for once, I quickly relinquished the responsibility to Lara. This, of course, made what happened partly my own fault. Monica, too, saw the chance to put her feet up and broadly gestured to Lara as she said, "Have at it."

Whenever Lara begs to plan an event, you should at least retain veto power or something. Otherwise, you get what we got last Sunday—CHICKS AT CHURCH.

I nearly died when I walked into the chapel and saw "Chicks at Church" printed on the neon-colored program. Even Brian, who loves a good gag, nearly gagged. Lara had refused to share any of the details with me because she was determined to make the meeting a surprise. It was.

I sat uneasily between Brian and our children as the "show" unfolded. Lara, who it turns out is not only a regular fan of the "Neighbors" show, but of every other talk show on the air, had come up with her own version of daytime television. Only the cameras were missing.

It started with Brother Powell as the announcer. "Brothers and Sisters, Welcome to 'Chicks at Church,' the talk show about today's Relief Society sisters. And now, your host, Lara Westin."

I could feel the heat on my neck already, and I scooted down into my jacket. Erica, Grayson, and Ryan looked over at me, realized their mother was in agony, and grinned.

"Welcome everybody!". . . Oooo-eeee. . . (There's nothing like the shrill blast of feedback to wake up the sleepers on the back row). Lara smiled as somebody adjusted the microphone to her enthusiastic volume. "'Women Who Love Too Much—Is That Really Possible?' Today, on 'Chicks at Church.'"

I winced. "I'm going to die here in this chapel with a run in my nylons," I whispered to Brian.

Lara went on. "Then, we'll talk about the Word of Wisdom Diet. Today, on 'Chicks at Church.'"

Brian whispered in my ear, "'Women Who Die at Church.' Today, on 'Chicks at Church.'"

"Shh."

But Brian wasn't through. "'Men Who Marry Women Who Die at Church. Today, on 'Chicks at Church.'"

I elbowed him. "Be quiet."

"'Men Who Marry Women Who Die at Church, and Then Marry Razorback Hogs.' Today, on 'Chicks at Church.'"

It was all I could do to stifle the laughter, and I gave him my most furious glance. Seeing he had me right on the edge of hysteria, he finally stopped.

"But first," Lara said, winking, "let's welcome your favorite and mine, the Chickie Baby Choir."

Immediately I calculated how long it would be, after coming home from church, before I'd get a phone call from a very unamused stake president. I could feel prickly little hives breaking out on my throat. My daughter, Erica, gave me the first woman- to-woman glance of sympathy I'd ever seen on her face.

Six of our elderly sisters (who probably hadn't been called chicks in sixty years) stood and sang to their hearts' content and my heart's torment. The song was all right, some upbeat number Lara had dug out of her piano bench. But the name of the group! "I will never live this down," I whispered to Brian.

"And now, a word from our sponsor," Lara said. Our *sponsor*?! I thought. Who is that going to be—Casseroles R Us?

"But you had nothing to do with it," Brian whispered back.

I gave him a look. He knew as well as I did that when you're president of an organization, all complaints float up to you personally. Even if Lara had masterminded the whole thing—and she had—I'd be the one blamed for it.

The sponsor, Meg White, our food chairman, was carrying a tape recorder. "Sisters, now you can visit teach the easy way, with Dial-A-Visit. For just $9.95 a month we'll call every sister on your route, and she'll receive the message from a Mormon celebrity."

A Mormon celebrity? My eyes were stretching wider by the minute. Meg fumbled with the switches, then we heard Meg's husband trying to fake an ancient voice. "This is Brigham Young," he wobbled.

"Oh, this can't be happening," I whispered. Brian squeezed my shoulders, trying to comfort me.

"Celebrity voices impersonated," Meg said.

No kidding.

"How many women will actually try that?" I hissed to Brian. "I'll spend the rest of my life explaining that it was just a joke."

"And that you weren't really trying to raise money," he whispered back. I closed my eyes.

On the stand, the bishop's counselors, who were conducting, sat in a frozen stupor. Occasionally they glanced at each other, but neither one knew whether Lara had crossed the line of acceptability or not—nothing like this had ever happened before. Without Bishop Carlson, no one knew what to do. Should they get up and close the meeting? Or should they just chuckle and see if things improved? They opted to chuckle, but things did not improve.

From the commercial, Lara went to a movie critic (a sister who had actually served ice cream made from mother's milk at a ward dinner the year before). She rated three current movies with telestial, terrestrial, and celestial ratings.

"Oh, no—it's that milk woman," Grayson whispered.

I took a deep breath and turned to Brian. "I'm going

to lie down and die now, darling. Please take care of the children and remember to feed the dog."

Brian chuckled. "Come on, it's almost over."

I looked at the clock. It was not almost over.

Next, Lara had two interviews about whether a woman can love too much (no) and the Word of Wisdom Diet (yes). The last guest was a book reviewer who recommended the Book of Mormon as this week's "chick pick"—a "terrific drama, filled with greed, corruption, lust, violence, love, and sweeping history."

For the first time in my life, I wished I were outside the chapel playing hall hockey with the rowdy boys who thought we couldn't hear them. Surely they'd let me into the game as soon as they took one look at my pitiful posture, my drooping face, my tear-stained blazer. Oh, why couldn't Bishop Carlson be here?

Finally Lara bid goodbye to all her faithful viewers, and the network signed off.

As we stood to leave, Brian smoothed my frizzy hair. If it had not already been standing on end, it would have been by the end of the meeting.

"See?" Brian said, "You survived, honey."

"Uh-oh," I whispered back. "Here comes Sister Delaney."

She was shaking her head as she made her way down the aisle.

"Sister Taylor," she said, suddenly formal. "Several women were very offended today." Her chin shoved its way up into the air.

What? She'd already had time to run around and survey the audience reactions? "Well, I'm still waiting for the Nielsen ratings to come in," I said, trying to kid with her.

"Oh. So you *approved* of what happened here tonight."

This was starting to feel like a no-win situation. "Uh," I said, "I'm not sure exactly *what* happened here tonight, to be honest."

"Well it's *your* organization. If you don't know what's going on, who does?"

Thank goodness Brian jumped in just then. "Sister

Delaney," he said, putting one arm around her, "You're just the person I wanted to ask about singing in the choir."

The old choir ploy. Thank goodness I married the ward choir director, whose very presence in the right situation could clear a building faster than a five-alarm fire.

"I'm entirely too busy for the choir," Sister Delaney said, and then got elbowed aside by a scrambling deacon.

"Oh, that was so funny. I just loved every minute!" somebody said. Sister Delaney frowned as she huffed off, and several others gathered around to say they'd never attended such an entertaining fireside. I deflected all compliments to Lara, and scooted out of the chapel with Brian.

"Don't let Rita Delaney bug you," he said. "She's an unhappy person, always looking to whine and criticize."

I sighed. "I just hate to be attacked."

Brian sang softly as we headed to the parking lot. It finally occurred to me that he was doing a hilarious Ricky Nelson impersonation, singing "You can't please everyone."

I laughed and gave him a hug.

Just then, Lara dashed up. "Oh, good, you're smiling. I just knew you'd like my surprise."

I grinned. "You're a kick in the pants, Lara," I said.

"That's what Jerry says." She laughed.

"Well," I said, "he's right." And let's just hope, I thought to myself, that Bishop Carlson agrees.

CHAPTER 6

HAVE CALLING, WILL TRAVEL

"Well, I've heard some pretty clever schemes to keep a bishop from going out of town . . ."

I cradled the phone against my shoulder as I stir-fried some red peppers. "Welcome home, Bishop," I said.

"Sorry I missed the premiere," he said.

"Sorry I missed your vacation."

He laughed. "Boy, you really got folks talking. My Ansafone tape was completely full when I got home."

"All good I hope."

"Well," he laughed, "most people don't expect quite that much fire at a fireside."

"I know," I said. "I really apologize for—"

"On the other hand, the peas are always cold for somebody at the ward dinner. You know?"

I did know.

Bishop Carlson continued. "Some of these people need more to do in their lives. They forget what the gospel is about, and they get all worked up over somebody's good intentions that turned out . . . a little, well, different."

"I know some people didn't like it," I said. "I take full blame. I should have been more involved—"

"Well, that could have made it even worse, of course."

Now he was teasing and I was beginning to feel better.

"You do pick the worst times to go on vacation," I said.

He laughed. "Don't I, though? What was it last time—the scouts got lost in that park or something?"

"It was a cemetery."

"That's right. Heh, heh . . ."

I closed my eyes, trying not to remember the phone calls I had gotten that time, simply because the bishop was away and several mothers didn't know who else to call. It seemed that the scouts, on their way to the foothills to camp, had chosen a most inopportune time to cut through a cemetery.

The cemetery was at the north end of the city. Just as they reached the dead center (no pun intended), that section of the city had an electrical blackout. The boys were already trembling in their little scout shoes when the streetlights, which, moments before, had cast a dim light on the tombstones, suddenly went black as an open grave. Fourteen imaginations ran completely wild. Kids were tripping over sprinklers, falling onto graves, screaming and panicking all the way to the pay phones, where they called their moms. Then their moms called me.

"I'm holding you personally responsible as the Relief Society president," one mother had yelled. She flatters me, I thought. I only wished I could command the power lines and the scouting program, as this woman evidently thought I could.

"To tell you the truth, I don't think the meeting sounded so bad," the bishop said, bringing me back to the present.

"Well, I guess you had to be there," I said.

He laughed again. "Lara meant well," he said. "Sounds like everyone got a pretty good sermon on love and the Word of Wisdom."

"I assume you're using the word 'sermon' loosely."

"Don't let this bother you," he said. "You've learned for next time, right? And the complainers will soon be on to something else."

There he had a good point. I may be headline of the week for now, I thought, but before long they'll be scolding the activities chairman or somebody else.

"Isn't it a shame," the bishop said, "that people can't just look past all this stuff to what the gospel of Christ is all about? They get so caught up in the trappings, the programs, the petty problems. If they could just get into the spirit of the thing, you know?"

I did know.

"Of course, as Relief Society president, your job is to change the hearts of the weaker women so that they'll cheerfully serve and love unconditionally."

I laughed. "Oh, is that all?"

"Remember, you have stewardship over them. If they don't make it to the celestial kingdom, it will be your fault."

We laughed. Thank goodness Bishop Carlson has a good sense of humor. But even with the humor I felt the weight of the responsibility.

I sighed. "I think I feel my guilt alarm going off."

"Guilt's a good thing," he said. "Keeps us on track."

"Yes, well, mine has buried me *under* the tracks."

"You'll do fine. Don't worry about the fireside thing. Besides, you have bigger problems to think about."

"Oh, please . . ."

"Seriously. I need you to look in on the Verdugos. I hear Marla is packing up and moving out."

"Not again!"

"Well, check it out. And I just got a call from the Hunts. Miriam's mother died, so she and Clyde have flown back East. Their oldest boy is eighteen, but I don't know if he can handle all the meals plus his college studies and work."

"I'll get right on it. And by the way, Sister Latham called. Her feet are swelling and she's supposed to keep them elevated, so I'm going to take a meal in tonight," I said.

"Great. Sure appreciate you."

"Thanks. I'll mark that down. Let's see, that's one in the Yes column."

He laughed. "Hang in there."

Two hours later, after dropping Erica off at gymnastics, Grayson off at piano, Ryan off at T-ball, and food off at Sister Latham's, I stopped in at the Verdugos'.

"Oh, Sister Taylor, I'm so glad you came to help me

pack," Marla sobbed. "I can't believe what a big job this is. It's just too much for one person alone."

Somehow, Marla seemed more upset about having to pack than about losing a marriage. She handed me a bowl to wrap, then stared at me incredulously as I put it on the counter. "Actually," I said, "I came to talk with you."

"Talk?! This is hardly the time for talking, Sister Taylor. I've got to pack before Gary gets home."

I glanced around the room. Little was disturbed except for the kitchenware. "You're trying to pack up all this furniture and move out before he gets home?"

Marla waved away the heavy stuff. "No, the big things can be done later. I'm just worried about the little stuff right now."

Suddenly I felt prompted to focus on what she had just said. "Marla," I smiled. "You just said something that might be the key to your problems."

She frowned. "I did?"

"Come and sit down with me, just for five minutes." I led her to a chair and prayed silently for inspiration. "Marla, you just said that you'll worry about the big things later, but that right now you're concerned about the little things."

"So?"

"So, sometimes we do that in marriage. Sometimes we forget the big picture—the overall goal—and we let the little, daily upsets crowd out the things that matter most."

Marla rolled her eyes. She looked so young. Her teens were but a breath behind her. "I was talking about *packing*," she said.

"I know you were. But there was a larger truth in your statement, and that's what I'm trying to get you to see."

Marla sighed and stood up. "I'm sorry, but I just can't sit here while you make mountains out of mole hills." She started packing again.

"But that's exactly what *you've* been doing," I said.

Now Marla whirled around, angry. "And how would you know anything about my marriage?"

I swallowed hard, then took a minute to find the right words. "Because I'm listening for inspiration."

Marla just stared. "Oh, please."

I smiled. "Marla, have you and Gary ever had a fight over something small, and at the time it seemed like everything was hopeless, but after you made up you saw how silly it all was?"

"Maybe. So?"

"So, when you first marry, it takes awhile to learn each other's language. It's easy to miscommunicate. And if you're not confident about your commitment to each other, every little bump looks threatening and scary. Those are the little things I was talking about."

Marla looked up, but kept wrapping dishes.

"When you feel confident about the permanence of your marriage, when you can really trust your mate, small disagreements don't look so large. No matter how strongly you disagree, underneath it all you still know the marriage will last."

"When does that happen?"

"With some couples, they never doubt. With others, it can take years for that doubt to disappear and be replaced by trust."

Marla stopped packing and tore off a paper towel to dab at her eyes.

"Marla, it's so easy to let the little things loom large when really they hardly matter," I said. "If little things make you feel that everything's hopeless, you need to work on the basics—the really important things that matter most."

"Like what?"

"Trust, for one. Living the commandments. Mutual respect. Testimonies. Putting the marriage first. Maybe you should talk to Gary about how insecure you feel in the marriage. If every little argument is making you take rash action, you need to build your faith in him, and in yourself."

Marla came and sat down. "Sister Taylor, how did you know that was how I was feeling? Is it because you're so much older?"

I sighed and then laughed. See, this is the thanks you get when you're Relief Society president—you really try to help people, then they ask you for a firsthand recollection of the Civil War.

"Now, see here," I said, still laughing. "I'm not all that old."

Marla blushed. "Sorry."

I patted her knee. "It's okay. When I was your age, I thought women over thirty were ancient. My kids think I grew up with the Pilgrims because I didn't have a VCR when I was little."

"You didn't?"

"Thanks a lot," I said.

Marla laughed. "Really, how did you know our problems were all because of little arguments?"

"Well," I said, "you tell me if I'm right. When you were growing up, your parents pretty much did everything for you, right?

"I guess so."

I winked at her. "You used to throw tantrums to get your way, and you never had to cook or clean. True?"

Marla laughed. "How did you know?"

"If you went to school without your homework, your mom brought it to you, didn't she?"

Now Marla's eyes grew wide. "Yes! How did you know that?"

"And if Gary doesn't pamper you the way you always have been pampered, you end up in an argument."

"He calls me the Mormon American Princess!"

"Are you?"

Marla looked sheepish. "Yeah, I guess I am."

"So, when Gary doesn't do what you want him to, you feel powerless. You don't know how to get through to him."

"Exactly!"

"So you pack up. It's just a bluff to scare him and get him to give in and pamper you, right?"

Marla's face filled with shame. "Is that what I'm doing?"

"Is it?"

She thought for a moment. "I guess I'm just so scared."

I stood up and put my arm around her. "Marla, if you throw a tantrum to get your way—and that's really what this is—pretty soon he'll start resenting it. You're manipulating him. Nobody likes that. Eventually, it's going to backfire."

"Gary says I'm playing games."

"You can fix this," I said. "You and Gary together."

"Do you really think so?"

"Absolutely. You need to believe that he loves you even when he refuses to pamper you. If Gary's smart, he wants you to be stronger and more independent than you're being right now."

"That's what he keeps saying."

"Hang onto him, Marla. Good husbands always admire strength in their wives. Now unpack those dishes and determine that whatever it takes to save the marriage, you're willing to do it. I have to leave now, but you can call me anytime."

Marla stood up as I headed for the door. "Aren't you going to help me unpa—" Then she stopped. "I mean, thank you for coming over."

I turned and grinned. "You're welcome."

Before driving off to pick up my children, I took a minute to sit in the car and pray my thanks for being able to talk with Marla. I'd had no idea what was going on there before listening for inspiration about the solutions she needed.

I hoped the Spirit would be as strong the next day when I had an appointment to see Jorja Willis.

Jorja opened the door as wide as her chain lock would allow, and spoke to me through the three-inch crack. It was not looking good, so I figured I'd go for the bold approach. "Hi, Sister Willis! May I come in?"

"For what purpose?"

This wasn't getting any easier. "Well, I thought maybe we could chat for a few minutes." I smiled and tried to look as harmless as possible. We had met a year ago, but that was B.P. (before perm) and maybe my new look caught her off guard, just as it did me each morning.

"You're probably here to try to get me to come back to church, but I'm not interested," she said.

Well, at least Sister Willis leaves no room for misunderstanding.

"That floozy is teaching Primary and I think it's a disgrace," she went on. "Because of her, I don't get to see my grandchildren. Now what kind of a church would allow such a woman to teach little children?"

I took a deep breath. "I guess the church of Jesus Christ."

"What's that supposed to mean?"

"Oh, Sister Willis, this is so hard to discuss on the porch. Couldn't I come in for just two minutes?" (Marla had agreed to hear me for five, but I figured I'd better knock it down a few minutes for Sister Willis.)

"No you may not. I've told you how I feel and that's final."

I sighed. "You must be an unusually strong woman."

"What do you mean by that?"

"I guess I always think people must be strong when they have been dealt a tough blow. And you have. I can't think of too many things harder than trying to forgive someone you feel has cost you so much."

"How do you figure that means I'm strong?"

"Because if you weren't strong, the Lord wouldn't have allowed it to happen. He said he won't ever allow us to be tried beyond our ability to withstand it. So . . . I just figure you must be stronger than most people."

Sister Willis frowned in the shadows. "You think the Lord did all this?"

"Oh, no, of course not. But he didn't intervene and stop it, because . . . I guess he knew you could conquer it. You know?"

"No, I don't know what you mean."

"I mean, no matter what terrible things happen to us in this life, we're promised that we can endure. We can forgive and somehow get through if we'll turn to the Lord for help."

"Well, I did pray to get my grandchildren back. And it didn't work. Their mother won't let them have a thing to do with me."

"That's so tragic. I really sympathize, Sister Willis. That's a gigantic loss on both sides, one that I'm sure she'll regret someday. But maybe, instead of praying to get them back . . . what about praying for the strength to cope with this loss—"

"And now you have that miserable woman who caused it all teaching Primary!"

"I know it's hard to forgive her. But there is repentance. Look how the Lord forgave—"

"So now you're siding with that floozy."

"I'm really not judging here. But if we can't forgive people, we're told that we'll be held as accountable as they will. It will be as if *we* committed those same sins."

"Ha! The day I'd run off with a married man!" Sister Willis rolled her eyes.

"See? You're strong in that respect. Maybe she was weak then. Maybe now *she's* strong." I shrugged.

"Fine time to get strong, after it's too late!"

"I know it's too late to save your son's marriage. But . . . it's not too late to save . . ." I stopped. Nothing sounded as intimate and caring as I was meaning it while I was standing like a salesman on the porch.

"To save what?" Sister Willis peered closer through the crack.

I shook my head. "It's really hard to talk to you here," I said. "I don't know you that well, but I . . . I just feel for you. I really do, Sister Willis. That was a crummy thing to have to go through."

"It certainly was."

"But you can control whether it stays crummy or if it gets a little better."

"What were you going to say that it isn't too late to save?"

"Well, what I was thinking might sound preachy or something." I looked away, feeling ridiculous for a minute, then decided I may as well tell her. "I was going to say that it's not to late to save your relationship with the Savior . . . that nobody can take your faith away."

"Don't talk to *me* about faith."

"Sister Willis, I honestly want to help you. Getting knocked down wasn't your fault. But *staying* down—that part you can control."

"Words," she muttered. "You haven't been through this."

"I hope I never have to, but if I ever do," I said, "I hope I can come to you for some help. I hope I can ask you how you overcame it."

Suddenly, Jorja slammed the door.

I thought about ringing the bell again to apologize. Obviously I had said too much or the wrong thing, or my specialty—both. Then, just as I raised my finger to her doorbell, I changed my mind and decided simply to write her a note in a few days. It started to rain as I headed back to my car.

This time, Andy, I thought as I drove home, you have really blown it. You will go down in history as The Relief Society President Who Couldn't Shut Up. I pictured Lara at my side. "You meant well," she would say. But meaning well just doesn't excuse this kind of clumsiness. Then I thought about Monica. "She never would've come back to church, anyway," Monica would say. But is any soul so lost as that? If only I were the right kind of president, I thought, I'd know the words to say that could make the difference, instead of getting doors slammed in my face.

My mind drifted to all the women I had counseled with and tried to comfort. The ones who seemed to be in the most pain were women whose own choices were causing their misery.

I thought about Jorja Willis and the pain she was feeling. It seemed new, kept alive somehow. Her present suffering seemed to be the result of her choice to stay angry. Oddly, Jorja's pain was probably more intense now than in years past because now the pain was coming from a sin on her part: the refusal to forgive.

Still, I couldn't help feeling partly responsible for her not coming to church. I felt I had heaped more misery upon that poor woman, when she'd had enough already.

So much for my grandiose goals: I may have helped Marla unlock some of the secrets to making her marriage work, but I probably motivated Jorja to buy a couple of

dead bolt locks. I still needed to talk with Claudia
Lambert, and Zan was coming to give her homemaking
night lecture that night. Things could only get better,
right?

CHAPTER 7

A SKELETON NAMED NICK

"Uncle Nick called while you were gone," Grayson said, without moving his eyes from the television. He was slouched down so far on the sofa that his chest was serving as a tray for his bowl of ice cream. "I heard his voice on the machine."

"Did you finish your homewor—"

"Totally. *And* my piano."

"Good. Now if we can just get Ringling Brothers to book a piano playing sea otter . . ." I pulled him up into sitting position.

"Hi, Mom. Can I go over to Kayla's house now?" Erica, having finished her thirty-minute babysitting duties, looked confident about what my decision would be. Her coat was already on and she wasn't even slowing down.

"If you're back by 5:30 for dinner," I said. "I have to go to homemaking tonight."

"No way!" Grayson protested, obviously able to receive certain signals through the blaring cartoon. "You can't leave us alone with Uncle Nick!"

"What—he's in town?" I pressed the button on the machine. As if gathered at an old radio to hear the announcement of World War II, my three kids were suddenly huddled beside me listening to the voice of my errant brother.

"Hi, Andy," he said. "Surpri-ise. This is Nick. I'm in town! Mind if I stay a couple of nights? I'll drop in at seven or so. *Ciao!*"

I don't know, but it seems to me that anyone who can't spell *ciao* shouldn't be allowed to say it. "Well, how nice! Uncle Nick is coming," I said, trying to sound buoyant. I turned and looked into the long faces of my children. They weren't buying it and neither was I.

"Mom, you're not really going to allow him to stay here, are you?" Erica gave me the same look she gives her gum-popping friends before they both mutter, "Gross!"

"Come on, Mom, you can't!" Grayson's hands were clasped in a begging position.

"Oh, you kids are so overly dramatic," I said, trying to pooh-pooh the calamity that was nearly upon us. "Uncle Nick is family. We can't just turn him away."

Grayson turned to Ryan, the only neutral country in the picture, and began organizing a resistance. "C'mon, Ry, you've gotta stick with us. We need your vote, man!"

This was more power than Ryan had enjoyed all week, so he basked in it for a moment, grinning. Then, flattered to be one of the big kids with an entire vote, he glanced at his comrades and said, "I vote No."

I laughed. "Well, this is not up for a vote. We *have* to let Uncle Nick stay. At least for a night or two."

Grayson's eyes were bulging like a dead cod's, and Erica was pretending to gag. "Just two nights. I promise," I said. Erica, sensing there was no chance that she could change her future, headed out the door to Kayla's house, hoping to find some sympathy there.

Grayson, mumbling about being doomed, led his new recruit, Ryan, over to the sofa to sulk about their defeat by their mother. I tried to hum cheerily as I made dinner so the kids wouldn't hear me moaning. I felt guilty about making them put up with Nick again. But I also knew I'd feel guilty about turning my back on my only brother. Maybe I'd get to work on Edith's guilt quilt tonight.

Last time Nick had visited, he had swept through the door wearing a cape and an aviator scarf. "It's Zorro!" Ryan had whispered, trembling.

Nick, who had never taken a drama class in his life ("Never needed one," Brian once observed) had announced that there was big money in community theater, his new love. He then went on to explain that, with proper backing from the right arts patrons, he could elevate the world to new theatrical heights. The words "Broadway" and "Tony" kept creeping up—words which had never passed his lips before.

Every time he breezed into town, he seemed to be running another scam. "I think he's fleecing people," I once whispered to Brian in bed, after an evening of hearing Nick talk about some twin-engine aircraft deal.

"What was your first clue?" Brian had said, wearily. "Let's face it, Andy. We're probably harboring a crook."

It just seemed so impossible that my baby brother, who won a state speech contest with a speech entitled, "Why I Love America," was now swindling his way through America's highways and byways.

"Under no circumstances are you to fork over one dime to that hustler," Brian had said years ago. And this was ten minutes after meeting the guy, when Brian and I were still dating. "He's as slippery as an eel," Brian had whispered.

Though he never asked us for any money, Nick constantly seemed to be honing his craft of fraudulence. In restaurants he would say to a French waiter, "Oh, where in France are you from?"

"Paris," the waiter would tell him.

"Ah," Nick would marvel. "From your accent, I would have guessed Dijon."

Brian and I would exchange tired glances and hope no one we knew was sitting at a nearby table.

The kids were fed up with his outrageous lies, too. "Did Uncle Nick really sell a diamond to the Queen of England?" Grayson had asked a few years before, as we were tucking him into bed.

"Do you hear Scotland Yard banging on our door?" Brian had asked.

"No."

"Well, then rest assured that Uncle Nick has never set foot in Buckingham Palace."

With heavy heart, I explained to the kids that Uncle

Nick was prone to exaggeration, but that we could still
love him. At first, he was a colorful storyteller, regaling
the kids with outlandish tales of gold mines, buried
treasure, and shoot-outs. (The shoot-outs may have been
genuine.) Then, when the kids realized it was all bogus,
they felt duped. Their heroic uncle was a charlatan and an
embarrassment. Having him in the house meant having
no friends over for fear of Uncle Nick launching into
another ridiculous fable.

It also meant having the phone ring at odd hours
during the night. Once a police car screeched up to the
door, sirens blaring, hot on Nick's trail for some kind of
forgery. "I am *majorly* humiliated," Erica had said. Nick
had left, and I had no clue where he was.

Then, three months after the incident, Nick called to
say the whole thing had been a practical joke played on
him by some wealthy investors.

"Right, Nick," I had countered, furious. "People buy
policemen all the time. You must think I'm a perfect idiot."

"Well, nobody's perfect, Andy." Nick was trying to
tease his way out of it.

"How dare you make me harbor a criminal," I snapped.
"I want you to clean up your act, or you can't stay here
anymore. You scared the kids to death. I'm not going to
protect you from the law, you know."

This is always when Nick offers the most beautiful
apologies you have ever heard. He sounds so humble, so
loving, so believable. With flawless logic he explains away
every suspicious detail. His voice oozes warmth and you
find yourself adoring the scoundrel, after all.

"He'll say whatever it takes to keep your door open,"
Brian said. "He's been conning you all your life."

It was true. Even as a child Nick was so convincing,
so slick, that he'd fool me over and over. I was nine years
his senior, but he was nine times smarter. "Maybe if I
hadn't been so gullible he wouldn't have become so
confident about his lies," I said.

Brian shook his head. "So now it's your fault that
Nick has become a phony? Gimme a break. The minute he
walks in, I smell snake oil. You smell guilt."

Brian was right, of course. I feel sorry for Nick because I'm the only member of the family who will speak to him. I was the oldest of four and I always felt guilty that that I didn't spend more time with Nick. By the time he was old enough to pal around with, I was a teenager with friends of my own.

Brian scoffs at these sentimental regrets. "Are you kidding? You practically raised your sisters and brother. If anything, Nick was the center of attention." Brian had talked with Nick on his last visit and told him that if he had even a feeling that things weren't fully honest in Nick's business schemes, he'd turn him in.

I'll never forget the scene: Nick's eyes filled with tears and he hugged Brian. "You are the best brother-in-law a guy could have," he said. "You really do care. To see how you protect my Andy . . . I am *so happy* she found you."

I have to admit, even my eyes were misting up. But Brian saw right through Nick's floral bouquet, and simply said, "Well, she's *my* Andy now, Nick. So watch it." After Nick had left, Brian turned to me and said, "We need to make you con-proof, honey. Those were crocodile tears if ever I've seen them."

That night I had felt so guilty for having made the family put up with Nick that I baked them the world's most decadent chocolate torte. Then, I felt so guilty about celebrating Nick's departure that I wrote and told Nick to come stay with us again sometime.

Dinner was almost ready when I heard Brian's car pulling into the driveway. Eager to report the impending crisis, Grayson bolted out the door and was slapping the fenders even before Brian had come to a stop. By the time he walked into the kitchen, Brian was giving me a look.

"Oh, come on, now," I said, looping my arm through his and taking his briefcase from him. "After that talk you had with Nick, I'm sure he'll be better behaved this time."

"He said *ciao* on the answering machine," Grayson tattled.

Brian swept his arms into the air on either side. "I rest my case. What is he pushing this time—Italian race cars?"

"I don't know, but I have homemaking meeting tonight. I have to be there. I invited Zan Archer to speak on investments."

"Oh, good," Brian said. "She can hold up a savings bond and say 'Yes,' then she can point to Nick and say 'No.'"

"I'm not taking him with me!"

"So what you're saying is, you're leaving us alone with the master of disguises. Twenty bucks says he shows up in a beret."

"Oh, you can handle him for one evening, Honey. I'll be back by nine."

"Ten and you know it."

"Okay, ten. By then you'll all be in bed and half of his visit will be over."

"Are you kidding? He'll just be warming up. Ten is dinnertime to people like Nick."

"Pleeeease?" I craned into Brian's face as I carried a steaming casserole past him.

Brian just shook his head. "My infernal companion," he mumbled.

"It's Nick's birthday next month," I said. "Maybe we should give him something."

"How about some restraint?"

I smirked. "Seriously, Brian, how many people do you think will remember him?"

"Probably half the residents of the poor house."

"I know! Have a family home evening tonight," I said. "There you go. Do something structured. It would be good for someone who travels as much as Nick does to hear some gospel truths."

"Nick is a fraud," Brian said. "There's a gospel truth for you."

"You know what I mean—in a family setting."

"Did it ever occur to you that this could be backfiring?" Brian stared upward as if the scenario were laid out before him on the ceiling. "Nick is a returned missionary, a serviceman with a distinguished record, and he's now thirty-two years old. Every time he visits, you hope that he'll see our happy little family and decide to settle down." Brian looked at me, grinning. "Maybe we're the reason he won't!"

I stopped, my eyes round with panic.

"I'm kidding, I'm kidding." Brian held me for a minute. "Just what you need—something else to worry about."

I sighed. "How was your day, anyway?"

Brian smiled. "It started a lot better than it's ending."

"I love you," I said. "You're a good sport. And a good father."

Brian took a giant strainer out of a drawer and held it over his face like a mask. Eyes darting, his mouth twisted into an evil grin, he said, "Those are always the ones who lose it someday." Then, in a falsetto voice, "He seemed like such a normal neighbor. You'd never think he would shove his brother-in-law through a strainer."

I laughed and pulled the strainer away from him. "You're the reason the kids are so weird sometimes." I dabbed butter onto the vegetables. "You'll be fine tonight. You'll think of something."

"I've already thought of something," Brian said. "Let's put a *sold* sign on the lawn."

CHAPTER 8

CAN I BORROW A CUP OF GUILT?

"You can't believe the crisis I left at my house," Monica said as I walked into the Relief Society room. "Brittany is having a sleepover and poor Art is stuck with a night full of giggling little girls."

I smiled, picturing the dour faces of my family and the trial *they* were in for that evening. Hey—maybe those girls would like to hear a good storyteller—nah, perhaps not.

"Edith says she's ready for her demonstration. Then we can go right into Zan's lecture," Monica went on. "Zan isn't here yet, but I'm sure she'll show up. Oh, and I asked Jill McPhee to say the opening prayer. Oh, listen, she's wearing a wig—don't say anything."

Just then, Jill came around the corner in what appeared to be a fright wig. She had combed most of it down, but some of the more stubborn pieces stuck out like sun's rays.

"Hi!" she chirped. She was probably the only woman in America who shared her silhouette with the Statue of Liberty.

"Hi, Jill," I said. "Great to see you." I hoped that she knew I meant it sincerely. Jill smiled, then went into the ladies' room.

Jill came out to church every six months or so, but the last time I had seen her, she had thin, wispy hair about the length of mine. This sudden billow of protein was quite an eye-opener. Monica went on to explain that, according to her sources, Jill had bleached her hair blonde and then suddenly it had all fallen out.

"Just don't say anything about it being a wig," Monica whispered.

"Oh, of course not," I sympathized. Poor Jill.

Just then I felt someone tap my arm. It was the new sister, Justine Overland.

"Hi, Andy. I meant to call and ask you if maybe I had the wrong date for the welfare farm. I got your map to the church here, but no one else showed up to carpool."

"What?" I wondered why she didn't drive directly to the farm, following the map I sent. Then it hit me. I had made a terrible mistake. When I was dashing out the door to help Marla Verdugo that first time, I must have sent Justine the map to the church. And that meant that I had mailed Zan a map to the welfare farm, forty miles away!

"Andy, are you all right?" Justine led me to a chair, where I slumped. I must have looked like I had just driven a less-active sister right out of the church. And if Zan was circling the parking lot of the welfare farm, cursing me this very minute, that's exactly what I had done. "Monica, we're going to have to show everyone a videotape in place of our speaker," I croaked. "I sent Zan a map to the welfare farm." I didn't even feel like mentioning that the stake Relief Society president and her second counselor had said they might visit our meeting that night.

"Oh, Zan will figure it out," Monica said. "I'll bet she gets here any minute. Let's go ahead and start."

I stood up to conduct. "Greetings, everyone," I said, pasting a smile on my face and trying to look composed. We sang the opening hymn, then I stood up and actually said, "Jill McWig will say our opening prayer."

Monica's eyes—*everyone's* eyes, Jill's most especially—popped open in surprise. I could read Monica's silent lips: "You said McWig!"

"Oh, Jill—I am so sorry. I meant Jill McPhee will say our opening hair. I mean prayer." By now I was ready for the vet to put me to sleep. I wanted to dash out of the room and run all the way home. Well, not home, because Nick would be there. Maybe I'd head north. That's it. No, I would probably run into Zan Archer heading back from the pear farm with my name written on her front bumper. I'd go south. No, I'd bump smack into the stake leadership on their way to see what a fine job we've done in what will probably be renamed Psych Ward.

Realizing that I could run but I could not hide, I determined to stay and tough it out. I apologized to Jill again, but she was decidedly cold. Monica announced that Jill was having a garage sale at her house in the morning. I made a promise to myself to go and buy something. Maybe I could smooth things over by being her best customer.

During the visiting teaching message, I slipped out to try to reach Zan Archer on the hall phone. No answer and no machine. I called Brian, but he hadn't heard from her either. The most he had heard about archers, he said, was that there were some amazing ones Nick had met on his last swing through Africa, who could pierce the hide of a wildebeest at five hundred yards.

There was nothing to do but wait.

I decided to go back in. At least there was one victory tonight: Edith was going to do a demonstration on unknown uses for common household products. Just having her come into the church building and teach a class was an amazing leap in itself.

I slipped in at the very moment Edith stood up. Glancing around, I noticed that the two stake leaders had just arrived too. They waved and smiled.

Edith stood before a table of surprises, which she had covered with a heavy cloth. As if unveiling a statue, she suddenly whisked off the cloth and actually said, *"Voila!"* Good grief, I thought, I ought to line her up with Nick.

Suddenly I heard everyone gasp. I peered around Lara and saw that on Edith's table was a bottle of vodka, a six-pack of beer, a box of tea bags, a pipe, and a wine rack.

If I hadn't been speechless I would have yelped. I glanced over at Monica, who looked as if she had just consumed all of the above.

"This cannot be happening," I whispered to Lara.

Lara patted my leg. "Let's just see what she says."

See what she says? What's to say? We're dead. I could feel the eyes of the stake leaders on me, so I glanced up, smiled and shrugged. Their eyebrows lowered.

Edith, meanwhile, had been quoting the Word of Wisdom, and explaining why all those items were bad for your health. Therefore, she concluded (thrifty soul that she is) when you give them up, they can be recycled rather than thrown away.

Of *course*, Edith, I thought. Why doesn't everybody think of that?

Several of the sisters were wearing pinch-lipped expressions and folding their arms tightly over their chests.

"Not many folks know this," Edith said, "but vodka will take paint off wood. Just think what it does to your stomach."

I could only imagine.

She then demonstrated by wiping the whiskers off a tole-painted wooden cat. If only vodka could erase an entire evening.

Next, she explained that while most people know beer makes a great hair rinse, few people use this bio-degradable marvel in the garden to control snails. "But," she said cheerily, "It'll kill those little buggers quick as a wink." And, lest any of us doubt this sage advice, Edith had brought along a bag of snails to demonstrate.

"She's killing those snails right here in the Relief Society room," I muttered. This was going to be right up there with Sister Delaney's dead cat lesson.

Next, Edith picked up the tea bags. "Ever get puffy eyes?" Edith said. "Well, slap these babies on, and your eyes will look rested in no time."

That's what I need, I thought. I need a giant tea bag for my entire body. By now everyone was laughing except me.

"As for any old tobacco pipes you may find around the house," Edith said, as if such discoveries were common to all, "just fill 'em up with dishwashing liquid and your kids'll have the best bubble blower in town." She then demonstrated, blowing happy little bubbles over all our heads. "And look," she continued, "I don't have to get my fingers all goopy with that little wand that comes in the bubbles bottle."

Well! There's reason enough to go out and buy a pipe, I thought. This whole thing is your fault, Andy, yours alone. You brought Edith onto the board. You mailed Zan the wrong map. You mentioned Jill's wig—twice.

Edith picked up the wine rack. "Now here's a versatile piece of equipment you'll be glad you saved. You can use hydroponics to grow plants in it, store firewood in it; fill it with jars of peaches, use it to organize your makeup, stick skeins of yarn in those holes if you knit; or at Christmas, you can stuff it with lights and garland, and make yourself a little ol' Christmas tree." Edith was beaming with pride over this last one.

Much as I dreaded getting a phone call from Zan, I actually felt a wave of relief when the hall phone started ringing and I had to leave the room to answer it.

It was Brian. "Zan called," he said. "She's pretty upset. She says she drove sixty miles."

"Oh, it's not sixty, Brian."

"Well, it seems she got lost on the way."

I groaned. "What more could go wrong?"

"Nick is filling in for her."

"Ha ha."

"I'm serious."

"What?!"

"I couldn't stop him. He knew you'd be short a speaker, so he jumped in his car and he's on his way."

I started to cry. "Brian, how can this be happening?"

"Do you want me to come down there?"

"No. I don't want you to leave the kids at night. It's raining and you know how Ryan always wakes up—"

"Listen, everything will be fine. Just tell the sisters to go home. They'll probably be glad to get home early in this weather, anyway."

I headed back toward the Relief Society room to try to catch Monica's eye, but Edith had just finished and the stake leaders were coming toward me. Sister Salisbury looked bewildered, but her counselor, Sister Garcia, was cracking up. "I have never applauded a homemaking lesson before," she said. "That woman should be a stand-up comic. I'm sorry we have to leave."

Sister Salisbury, gentle to the core, tried to express her confusion as lovingly as possible. "I realize we can learn a lot through humor," she began. "But I just don't feel comfortable about seeing all those items in our building. I did like her point that we shouldn't *consume* those things . . ."

Sister Garcia nudged her. "C'mon. I'll explain the jokes to you on the way home." And then to me, "No wonder your attendance has risen." Thank goodness they thought Edith was joking.

I tried to chuckle as I waved good-bye, but my smile froze as I saw Nick drive up. He screeched up to the curb and leaped out like a paramedic at an accident scene. Actually, I could have used a paramedic right about then.

"Hi, Andy! Hey, great hair!"

I quickly glanced behind me to make sure Jill wasn't standing there getting yet another insult. The coast was clear. No, Nick seemed genuinely impressed with *my* new look. (It probably reminded him of some exotic, red-crested boobie he'd seen through a pair of binoculars somewhere.)

At any rate, he did seem thrilled to see me, and I have to admit I do love the rascal. We hugged.

"Nick, you can't teach Zan's lesson—"

Nick was already jogging into the building. "Sure I can. I know all about investments. You name it, I can lecture on it. What do they want to know about—the Yen? Portfolio tips?"

"Nick, wait!"

He was gone. I ran after him. We are in serious trouble, I told myself. Monica pulled me aside just as I was about to grab Nick's coat.

"Where's Edith and that vodka?" she whispered. I laughed. "Why don't you go in and give a lecture on how your calling has driven you to drink?"

Monica leaned against the wall and slowly started sliding down it. "This night is such a disaster I can't even believe it."

"Well, believe it," I said. "And it's also about to get worse."

Monica scrambled to her feet again and followed me into the Relief Society room. But we were too late. Nick was already running the show and even had the lectern on the table as if stumping for an election.

Monica and I sat in stunned silence and listened to one of the best darn talks we'd ever heard. At least we *think* that's what happened. Later, we both agreed that we must have been in shock, so who knows what Nick really said. But at the time, he sounded almost solid. I couldn't believe it.

He talked to the women about common checking penalties they could avoid, what to do if their purse was stolen, little-known tax breaks, clever mortgage ideas, differences in credit card rates, home equity loans, insurance premiums, and finally how to avoid phony get-rich-quick schemes. I couldn't believe it.

"I thought Nick was that weird brother we met last January," Monica whispered.

"He is," I said. "I guess . . . I guess Nick just has a lot of information on a lot of esoteric subjects."

Monica and Art had bumped into us at a restaurant the last time Nick visited. Nick had shaken hands with Art and said, "There's a man of health and vigor—the two most important characteristics in buying chickens, I might add."

My mouth had dropped open and Brian had closed his eyes. But Nick went on. "Hens in good laying condition have bright red wattles and waxy combs. In yellow-shanked breeds, the beak and shanks are pale yellow or white. The skin of a good layer is soft and pliable, and the back is wide and long."

Monica giggled and glanced at Art's back side.

"Molting is important, too," Nick said. "Poor layers usually molt earlier than good ones. Molting shouldn't occur before September or October."

Monica took a closer look at Art's hairline, and we all forced a courtesy laugh.

"Nick is the family almanac," Brian said, trying to explain the unexplainable.

"Yes, Mother tried to make him right-handed," I teased.

Nick chuckled, then said, "Well, just remember that information next time you go to buy chickens."

"Yes. We certainly will," Art said. Then he and Monica had beat a hasty retreat.

"Nick," I said, "by any chance are you gathering investors for a poultry business?"

He laughed at the preposterous suggestion. "Poultry business . . ." he mumbled, savoring the humor in my question. "Of course not." He took a bite of his salad. "Everybody knows the real money today is in eggs."

This time *I* closed *my* eyes.

And now, here he was, egg expert extraordinaire, charming the sisters of the ward, and looking like Dr. Dollar, that brainy economist on the evening news.

"You liked my speech. I can tell." Nick gave me a hug.

I finally closed my mouth and swallowed. You have to be quick to compliment Nick before he does it himself. "Yes. You really saved the day," I said. "Thank you, Nick."

In a sweeping flourish, Nick bent low to kiss my hand. "That's what brothers are for," he said. "Big sisters are for letting you stay over when you're in town." He grinned. "Thanks."

"Big? Hmm . . . I'm not sure I like your choice of words."

"Okay," Nick said. "Older sisters are for—"

"Let's go back to big," I said.

Monica, still in a daze, wandered out into the hall. Just then, Zan Archer came storming through the other door, eyes blazing.

"Oh, Zan—I am so sorry—" I began.

"YOU GAVE ME THE WRONG MAP!" she yelled.

Terrified, I squeezed Nick's hand. "Oh, I know," I said. "I made such a mistake. Please forgive me, Zan—"

"This is Zan?" Nick said, turning.

And then it was as if a soundtrack of violins suddenly

came on: Zan and Nick locked glances and stood there, blushing like children as they stared into each other's eyes.

"Hello," Zan murmured, extending her hand.

"Nicholas Butler." *Nicholas*?! Then he took *her* hand and kissed it.

I gasped. It was one thing for Nick to kiss *my* hand. I'm his sister. I grew up with his dramatics. But this—this courtly groveling and trance-like staring—this unabashed display of fairy-tale infatuation—I was disgusted. And Zan, a professional, a corporate tiger type, suddenly melting and going all gooey and falling for Nick's act. It was simply too much.

I started to apologize to Zan again (and to simultaneously motion to her not to believe Nick for a second), but she had forgotten I was there.

Nick launched into one of his blue ribbon apologies in my behalf, and before he had finished, Zan was purring that everything was quite all right.

"But what did you do about the lecture?" she asked.

"Oh, Nick filled in," I said. "It really was great of him to do that without any time to prepare—"

Nick blushed and confessed to knowing a "tad" about finances. Simultaneously Zan and Nick began speaking "dollarese" to each other. Nick, the epitome of arrogance, was suddenly the picture of humility. And Zan, the take-charge dynamo who had just been screaming about my map, was suddenly swept off her feet into a fuzz of giggles and compliments—all directed at my brother, of course. I watched this entire nauseating scene play out right beneath my nose. Had I not witnessed it personally I never would have believed it. How could two such opposite people be so magnetically attracted to each other?

Would Zan discover Nick's game and later be even madder at me than ever? Would Nick get his heart broken by a self-described workaholic who had no room in her life for a man? I wondered if I should tune in tomorrow or just tune out altogether?

Realizing that neither Nick nor Zan were aware of anyone in the room but each other, I slipped out. Later,

Zan apologized to *me* for being so irate about the mix-up. "To tell you the truth," she said, "I was embarrassed to have driven so far before it occurred to me that I must have the wrong map. I haven't been to church for so long that I forgot how close the wards usually are."

When I walked into the bedroom that night, Brian was sitting up in bed, reading. "Oh, somebody called for you," he said. "They wanted to borrow a cup of guilt."

"Sorry. I'm fresh out."

"What? No worries?"

I told him the whole story. Nick and Zan had decided to go have a piece of pie together. Brian couldn't believe it. "Shall we call 911?" he asked. "I thought you said Zan was this . . . brilliant, savvy woman who—"

"I did. And she is."

"She *was*. She's getting Nicked as we speak. Every giant has a weak spot, Andy. While she's finishing off her pecan pie, Nick will be finishing off her portfolio."

"Do you think I should warn her? I mean, I do love my brother, but what if he gets her involved in some scheme?"

Brian shook his head. "Never mess with chemistry. Something could blow up."

I sat on the bed. "I guess you're right. I mean, if she's such a successful businesswoman, she should be able to figure it out for herself, right?"

During the night I got Ryan a glass of water and glanced out the window. Nick was standing on the back porch, wrapped in a blanket and staring at the sky. I considered going out and talking to him, but then thought better of it.

The next morning, a new Uncle Nick greeted the kids at breakfast. There was no bragging, no wild adventure stories of going over waterfalls, and no tales of elaborate financial schemes designed especially for congressmen. There was just a starry-eyed little boy in a robe.

"What's wrong with Uncle Nick?" Erica whispered to me in the kitchen.

"Whatever it is, I like it!" Grayson said.

I laughed. "I think Uncle Nick met someone he likes."

Erica wrinkled her nose. "And they like him back? No wonder he's in a daze."

"You sound like your father," I whispered. It was nearly a quote, as a matter of fact.

Then *I* was nearly in a daze because Nick offered to do the breakfast dishes. He even hummed as he worked. And then, the joyous announcement Brian and the kids had been waiting for: Nick had to be on his way and couldn't stay a second night. They all groaned in disappointment—an act Nick always buys. But this time Nick looked as if he were wise to their maneuvers, and even winked at me. "I have some business to wrap up," he said.

I walked out to his car with him. "Nick, are you all right? You're acting kind of . . ."

He smiled. "I know," he said. "Meeting Zan was . . . it really made me think about my life. My future." It was the first time Nick has said the word "future" without an "s" on the end.

"Already? I mean, you just met last night—"

Nick gave me a hug. "I know. But something clicked inside me the minute she walked in."

Oh, please don't let it be coins, I thought. "You mean when she was hollering about the wrong map."

Nick laughed as if Zan were the cutest little tease in town. "Yes," he said. "She swept me off my feet."

"She's a beautiful, bright woman, Nick—"

"Why do I feel there's a 'but' at the end of that sentence?" Nick said, and then smiled. "I already know what you're going to say—that Zan is married to her work."

"She told you that?"

"She said she's never met a man who was more exciting than her work before. And that's the same reason why I've never settled down. I've never met a woman who awakened in me that desire to make a commitment. Suddenly I want to change careers, be a family man . . ."

"With Zan? You guys are already talking about marriage?"

"No. Well, yes, sort of. I'm not sure it will be with Zan. I just know that it's alive in me. That feeling is there.

If Zan can awaken it, maybe there are other women who could too."

I was relieved.

"Or maybe not."

I began to worry again.

"Maybe Zan is the one," Nick continued. "Anyway, I need to do some serious thinking."

"Oh, please, Nick. Don't rush into anything. You've been so . . . so . . ." I wanted to say that he'd been so carefree for so long that he certainly didn't need to hurry now. But Nick interrupted.

"So weird for so long . . ." he said. "I'm getting so tired of all this. I really do believe in the gospel, Andy."

"I know that, Nick."

"And so does Zan."

"She does?"

"Absolutely. She just needs to get her priorities straight. She's allowed her career to consume her. And she knows it."

Nick kissed me on the cheek. "I'll be in touch," he said.

"Like always?"

He grinned. "Better than always."

I smiled and waved goodbye to two Nicks. One of them was backing down my driveway. The other one was gone forever.

CHAPTER 9

LOVE MEANS HAVING TO SAY YOU'RE SORRY . . . ON A REGULAR BASIS

That morning I was determined to drop by Jill McPhee's garage sale. So after taking the kids to school I drove over to Lark Avenue. We had visited her as a presidency several months before so I didn't take her address with me. But as I looked at the rows of nearly identical houses, I wasn't sure which one was hers.

Finally I saw it and pulled over. Tables of junk spilled out from the garage and down the driveway: rusty tools, broken chairs, racks of old clothing, and a playpen full of dusty toys. Two lamps with bent shades were leaning against a wooden ladder, and behind that were several stacks of dishes and books. A woman was rearranging some paint cans and fertilizer bags as I walked up the drive. Must be Jill's mom, I thought.

"Hi there," I called out.

"Can I help you?"

"Oh, I'll just browse around awhile," I said, patting an old electric mixer. "My mom used to have a mixer like this. I can almost smell the cookies!"

The woman just stared, so I cleared my throat and began looking through a box of record albums. "Oh, remember Three Dog Night?" I said. "Boy, this really takes me back. Beach boys . . . Moody Blues . . . The Supremes!" Swept away in nostalgia, I picked up a slender vase and sang into it, pretending it was my microphone. "Stop! In the-uh name of love . . . before you break my heart . . . Think it o-o-over . . . Remember that one?" The woman was still just staring at me. I chuckled nervously and put the vase down. Maybe I'd better buy something and be on my way, I thought.

"Hey, tennis rackets!" I said. "My two boys want to take lessons this summer and these would be perfect rackets for them to start with. How much do you want for them?"

"They're not for sale," the woman said.

"Oh." I put them down and started looking through her books. She had some wonderful old church books in the stack. "How much for the books?"

"I just said nothing is for sale here. Listen, I don't know who you are, but you can't just come poking through my things. I'll have to ask you to leave."

"What? Isn't this Jill McPhee's garage sale?"

The woman's eyes narrowed into slits. "This is *not* a garage sale," she growled. "This is my *private home.*"

I gasped, inhaling what must have been every bit of air in the entire zip code. Then I clamped my hand over my mouth. How could I have insulted that poor woman like this? "Oh, I am so sorry! Please forgive me. Oh, I am so embarrassed." My face must have been as maroon as Edith Horvitz's lips.

The woman kept glaring as I sprang into my van and zoomed out of there as fast as a van can zoom. I was still crouched over the steering wheel, cringing in embarrassment, as I rounded a curve in the road and saw Jill McPhee standing on the lawn of another house. Her yard was filled with customers, bed frames, golf clubs and knick-knacks.

I tried to swallow my humiliation. "Hi, Jill," I called. She tossed me an icy glance. I said to myself, "Hey. You just had a miserable experience a block away. Go home, make a hot fudge sundae, put your feet up and watch a game show."

But I had to try once more to mend things with Jill. "Please," I said, touching her arm. "Please forgive me, Jill. I'm such a klutz sometimes."

She lowered the frost setting and began to listen.

I continued. "I'm sorry about your hair. I mean—look at mine!"

Jill tried not to smile, then grinned despite herself. "Okay," she said. "You know about hair disasters. To be honest, I thought *you* were wearing a wig too."

"I wish!" We laughed. "Jill, I never meant to embarrass you. I was trying so hard not to mention your wig, that it's all I could say." I shrugged, begging her with my eyes.

"I guess I didn't really fool anyone."

"Well, no. But I didn't have to make matters worse. Please don't hate me forever."

She put her arm around me. "It's all right. I felt better when I saw Edith Horvitz's hair."

"Please come back to church again," I begged. "I'd just die if I thought I had made you so uncomfortable—"

"Hmm . . ." she said. "Can I grow my hair out first?"

"Hey, am I waiting until mine grows out?" We looked at each other and laughed.

"Okay. Maybe I'll come this Sunday. If you promise not to fix your hair first."

"How can you fix this?" I said, scrunching my frizzy coils with my hand. "At least you can hide yours under a wig. With you, me, and Edith, we probably look like the Nuclear Fallout Ward. Can't you just see investigators asking if there's something in our water?" Then we laughed again, and I told her about my awful blunder up the street.

"Wait a minute. That's Claudia Lambert's house," Jill said.

"No!" I slumped into a rocking chair. Claudia Lambert was the third woman we were trying to reactivate, the one whose house was so messy people had called the police. Now I had insulted her yet again.

"This can't be," I said. I should have figured it was someone in the ward when I saw the stack of old church books.

"Boy, you're really batting a thousand," Jill said. "If I were you, I'd move out of state."

I whimpered as I stood up. "Oh, come with me, Jill. Don't let me apologize to Claudia Lambert all by myself."

My new buddy laughed. "No way. You're on your own

with *that* woman. She's a real bearcat. Besides, I have to sell all this stuff."

"Please . . ." I whined. "I'll buy a headboard or something?"

Jill shook her head. "Here. You can have this pogo stick for your boys. It's on the house."

"Thanks." I took the stick and headed toward my van. A Cadillac had boxed me in, and I could see I wouldn't be able to get out.

"Oh, do you want me to move my car?" a woman called.

"No, that's okay. I'll come back in a few minutes." Why cost Jill a possible sale, I figured. I could just walk down to Claudia's. By the time I got back, the Cadillac might be gone anyway. Or, better yet, maybe someone would think my old klunker was part of the garage sale and buy it.

Every step was agonizing. It seemed all I'd been doing lately was apologizing to people. Maybe I could have Nick write up a few zinger apologies for me and hand them out as flyers.

Slowly I crept back up Claudia's driveway. She was dumping a box of old shoes into a garbage can. When she saw me, she started heading into the house.

"Sister Lambert, wait!" I shouted. She turned, startled that I knew her name.

"I am truly sorry about thinking this was a garage sale," I said. "There is really no excuse for it. I was looking for a garage sale at one of your neighbors, and . . ." I sighed. "I'm just really very sorry."

"How do you know my name?" she asked.

"I was telling Jill McPhee about the terrible mistake I made here, and she said this was your house. I'm the Relief Society president, so I recognized your name from the ward list."

"You tell her you tried to sing like Diana Ross?"

I could feel heat creeping onto my cheeks. "No. I left that part out."

Now Claudia started snickering. Her eyes began to water and soon she was howling with laughter. "You have more guts," she said.

I took a deep breath. She was not making it any easier.

Finally her laughter subsided and she looked me over. "Mind if I ask you a question?"

"Ask away," I said. By now I was so stripped of pride, no question could upset me.

"Did you hop over here on that pogo stick?"

"Oh!" I sputtered, throwing the thing down on the ground. "Of course not!" I was so flustered, all I could do was cry and laugh at the same time. "Sister Lambert, you must think I'm an absolute clown."

"You certainly make an interesting first impression."

"Yes, well, stick around. It gets worse."

Then Sister Lambert turned serious and pointed a finger at me. "Wait a minute," she said. "I know why you looked familiar to me. I saw your whole presidency on that 'Neighbors' show!"

Just my luck. No wonder she hasn't come to church. "That was an accident and I can explain," I said, sounding like a juvenile delinquent pleading with a policeman.

Sister Lambert hesitated, then threw caution to the wind. "Oh, what the heck. Come on in and tell me about it. Normally I'd say forget it, but . . ." she glanced at the pogo stick. "This has gotta be good."

So in I went where no Mormon had set foot in more than a decade. Sure enough, she could have used a cleaning crew and a neutering clinic for her cats. But after sitting down and laughing with her about the TV show, her surroundings faded away and I found Claudia Lambert thoroughly engaging.

"Okay, I'm going to top you," she said. Then she told me the whole story about how the police came when she was in a towel, and how the Relief Society sisters came to clean her house and that she did, indeed, threaten to shoot them. "I know it's a mess," she said. "But some folks are fat, and nobody comes over and wires their jaws shut for them. Just leave me alone with my own problems, I always say."

"We all need to work on certain things," I agreed. "As a matter of fact, I could use *my* jaws wired shut every time I say the wrong thing."

We talked some more and Claudia surprised me. She hadn't become inactive because of the police thing. Sure, she was mad for awhile, but the real reason was that she felt life had just dealt her too many rough blows and people in the ward weren't sympathetic enough. Claudia was a classic case of a woman imprisoned by self-pity.

"You don't know the experiences I've had," she said when I finally felt brave enough to invite her to church. "My father died when I was only fourteen."

I groaned. What a blow that must have been. I knew her feelings at once because my own dad had died when I was twelve.

"My mother criticized me the whole time I was growing up."

I pictured Claudia being ridiculed as she grew up. And then it hit me that the pain I was imagining was my own. My mother *still* criticized me. It always hurt when I was young, but over the years I had learned to just give her a hug and change the subject.

Claudia went on. "I went through a terrible divorce. My husband lost his job and left me with a stack of bills." On and on she went, listing health problems, broken trusts, wayward children, and every other heartache she had endured.

"See?" Claudia said. "You can't possibly understand what I've been through."

I took a deep breath and asked if I could tell her a couple of stories, too. Her eyes grew round with amazement as I spoke. I told her about some of the worst problems I had had in my life.

"But you seem so unaffected by the things *you've* been through."

"It's attitude," I told her. "Actually I am very affected by every problem I've had. I don't just walk off whistling, Claudia. I've cried buckets that nobody even knows about. But there comes a time when you finish. You learn what you can and get on with your life."

"And then those experiences help you deal with other people, I guess."

"Actually," I said, "it can make it harder if you don't get rid of all the self-pity."

"Huh? How?"

I smiled. "Well, having trials certainly makes us more sympathetic to people in genuine pain because there's a certain similarity in all suffering. You learn to recognize an aching heart. But it can also make us . . ." I searched for the right word, ". . . impatient with those we feel are weak. Whenever we think we've had it tougher than everyone else, we lose our sympathy for people who let the slightest problems overwhelm them. We compare. Then we get irritable because to us their complaints seem so trivial."

Claudia nodded. "Boy, do I know what you mean."

"But you can never tell what's upsetting to someone else," I said. "Maybe their problems look like nothing to us, but then maybe the things that bother *us* might be easy for *them* to endure. It's all relative."

Claudia paused. "I tried to come back to church a long time ago. But even though people were friendly, it just didn't seem to be enough."

"You have to let people get to know you," I said. "Some people are friendly the minute you meet them. Others are shy, and you have to be visibly *there* each week before they feel able to come up and embrace you, Claudia." Then I winked. "Or maybe it's *their* first time out, too, and they're waiting for *you* to come say hello to *them*."

She smiled weakly. "You know, one time I heard some sisters gossiping about me."

"Only once? What luck! Claudia, I guarantee you, if you get involved in PTA, church, business, you-name-it, you're going to hear some gossip. People are human, and the gospel net gathers all kinds of fish. Just because Christ's principles are true doesn't mean people become perfect when they get baptized. I guarantee that you'll get your toes stepped on if you come out to church."

"How can you say that?"

"How can I lie to you and say everyone will be perfect? They're simply not. Hey, with my luck, *I'll* probably be the one who does the toe-crunching!"

Claudia laughed.

"But," I continued, "the measure of our character is this: Do we let petty problems drive us away, or do we learn to forgive and come to church because we believe in the basic principles of the gospel?"

"I guess you really can't judge the church by every person you meet there."

"Claudia, every one of us has been gossiped about, or betrayed by people we thought were our friends. If it happens in the church, you just have to figure that those people are *social* Mormons. They eat Jello salad and well-done meat, but they don't understand what the gospel is *really* about." Claudia laughed, and I continued. "They need a change of heart." Then, with a wink, "And it wouldn't hurt them to change their menu once in awhile either." Claudia chuckled, nodding.

"So you have a choice," I continued. "Do you run away as if the approval of those few mean everything? Or do you go back and model for them the right way to treat people? I think you ought to show them how to be a true Christian."

"I don't know if I'm that strong yet."

"Well, it sounds like a pat answer, but the real truth is that you get strength from fasting and praying. If you want strength, you go to the source—Christ. Whenever I've felt hurt, I've drawn as close to him as I could."

"And that helped you forgive people?"

"Yes, but it's just like any family. It's easier to get along with some than others. And most of them really go the extra mile for you." What more could I say?

She nodded, listening. And then, without even knowing what I was saying, I found the very words she needed to hear. "Claudia," I said, "when you come to church with an empty cup waiting for others to fill it, you will never know the happiness that could come if you brought a full cup to church and tried to fill everyone else's."

She stared at me for a minute, then her eyes glistened with tears. "I guess I've just been waiting for everyone else to reach out to *me*."

I put my arm around her. "The answer is to turn that around," I whispered.

Claudia thought for a minute, then took a deep breath. "Thanks, Andy." She squeezed my hand, then laughed. "You seemed like such a nut at first."

"I know. Part of me *is* a little nutty, Claudia."

She laughed again and we hugged. I promised to visit soon. The very next Sunday, both Jill and Claudia came to church.

MOTHER OF THE YEAR

Monday morning I dreamed I was being chased by wardrobe colorists screaming my color season at me and waving swatches of fabric in my face.

At 7:30, workmen arrived to begin demolishing the east end of our house. This is what puberty is all about, I thought, as I pulled on some jeans and a sweatshirt. It isn't about hormones, pimples, or hairy legs. It's about spending thousands of dollars so that your only daughter can have her own bedroom, a canopy bed, and privacy away from her two beasty little brothers who would love nothing more than to pull a training bra out of her drawer and use it as a Ninja mask for one of their teddy bears.

"This is where I want the new entrance to the walk-in closet," I told the workmen. "This other door can be walled up." Erica was inheriting my closet and I wasn't even dead yet. Actually, I was kind of tickled to be giving her my big closet. I would have loved such space when I was her age.

Emptied of all my clothes and shoes, it looked suddenly much larger. Or, I thought to myself, I could just use this little room for storing all my unfinished homemaking crafts. I'd always wondered what people do with those.

"Where do you want this metal thing?" One of the workmen was trying to move a giant tin of honey—the kind that mysteriously appears in various closets and cubbyholes around our house. Our year's supply of food storage was crammed so tightly into our pantry that an extra tin of honey had no chance whatsoever of finding a home there.

"Next to the dresser is fine for now," I said. "The house is haunted by a former home management teacher."

"Huh?"

"Never mind." I made breakfast for the kids, put on my makeup, then went back into the kitchen. Ryan and Grayson had been trying to assemble their own school lunches lately, and every condiment in the refrigerator was scattered on the counter. "Hey, guys, clean this up before the Irish Republican Army calls and claims credit for it, okay?"

"Mom," Ryan asked, "in 'Pop Goes the Weasel,' does the weasel really explode and get blood and guts all over?"

I sighed, my own desire for breakfast suddenly gone. "No," I said.

"See?" Ryan smirked to Grayson.

I gave Grayson a look.

"Hey—you ruined 'This Little Piggy Went to Market,' so how is this any worse?" Grayson asked me.

"What do you mean, I ruined 'This Little Piggy Went to Market?'" It was entirely too early in the morning for me to deal with these deeper philosophical issues.

"When you told me the pig was going to market to be butchered," Grayson said. "Before you ruined it, I always pictured the piggy dressed up in a little hat and coat with a basket over its arm, like it was going shopping. And then you told me that the fattest piggy goes to market to be killed."

"I doubt very much that I said the word 'killed,' Grayson."

"Well, something like that. Anyway, I never liked that poem after that."

"That is hardly child abuse," I said in my defense. "And I'm sorry I ruined the poem for you."

I turned to Ryan, who looked as if he'd lost his best friend. "You mean the piggy isn't going shopping?"

"Oh, come off it, you two. It's a story about a farmer who has to take his pigs to market to earn a living. Some aren't ready, so they stay home where they can be fattened up."

"So they're not eating roast beef at a table?" Ryan asked.

"Have you ever seen a pig eat at a table?"

"I pictured it with a white tablecloth and everything," Ryan said, his eyes full of hurt and accusation.

"I hope you can find it in your heart to forgive me for telling it like it is," I said. "That's farm biz."

"I think it's terrible," Ryan said.

"Well, remember that next time you ask for bacon or sausage," I said.

"I'm never eating bacon or sausage again."

"I can't believe this conversation," I said. "Do you both have your T-ball outfits ready for the game this afternoon?"

"Mom, they're not called *outfits*. They're called *uniforms*." Grayson was rolling his eyes.

"Oh, pardon me," I said, dramatically. I was reminded of their last game when I had walked up behind the dugout and said in the most enthusiastic voice I could muster (given the fact that we were getting trounced), "Okay, Padres, let's get out there and make some points!" Grayson had gotten off the bench and shamefully approached his mother to tell me that they're called runs, not points. I apologized, then took a seat in the bleachers.

Ryan had later asked if the "T" in "T-ball" stood for "Tee-lestial."

"Yes," said Grayson. "It's the kind of ball where mothers are allowed to call you 'honey' in front of your teammates."

These are the boys whose mission farewells were to be displays of lavish praise for the mother who made them what they are today. I'd seen it in fantasy a dozen times. I'd stand and tell the darling baby stories every nineteen-year-old loves, then my adoring sons would step to the microphone and regale the congregation with examples of my phenomenal mothering skills. They'd recall the pancakes I made in the shapes of dinosaurs, the fact that I had never missed one of their T-ball games, the infinite hours I spent making flannelboard figures for family home evening. Their eyes would moisten as they recalled the extra helping of dessert they'd get when they'd had a rough day, the number of diapers I changed for them (rounded to the nearest hundred), and the scriptures I'd read to them. Each boy would choke up as he remembered the countless miles I drove so they could play sports and take piano, the bedtime stories and back-scratches, the homemade ice cream on every birthday—

"Mom, you forgot the sticker on my napkin yesterday."

—and the stickers I put on their lunch napkins every day but once.

Grayson was standing with his hands on his hips.

"We'd better call the napkin police," I said, tousling his hair. I finished packing their lunches, including Ryan's peanut-butter-and-potato-chip concoction, kissed Brian good-bye, and piled the boys and Erica into the van.

"Isn't it nice to have homemade ice cream on our birthdays?" I said as we drove along.

"Huh? Whose birthday is it?" Ryan asked.

"It's not anybody's birthday today."

"Then why are you talking about birthdays?" Erica asked.

I sighed. "I'm just saying that when it *is* someone's birthday, isn't it nice to have homemade ice cream?"

"What is she talking about?" Ryan whispered to Erica.

"We've never had that on our birthdays," Grayson said.

"You kids have it every birthday!" I said.

"We do?" Ryan and Grayson in unison.

"That's *homemade*?" Erica asked. "I wondered why it was always so runny on our birthdays."

I decided to try again. "Well, let's talk about the pancakes we have in our family. Isn't it fun to have them in different shapes?"

"We have pancakes in shapes?" Ryan was truly baffled.

"Oh, come on, you kids. We always make our pancakes into different shapes."

"I thought it was because you didn't know how to make round ones very well," Grayson said.

"Oh, never mind," I snapped. So much for cozy rituals. My fantasy of my children's mission farewells had suddenly changed. Ryan's talk would begin, "Except for the fact that we had to have ice cream and pancake tutors come over every week, I guess my mom was okay."

"If only she hadn't come to all my games and embarrassed me in front of my teammates," Grayson would say. "And then there was the time she ruined 'This Little Piggy Went to Market,' and turned me into a vegetarian."

I'd be waiting for them to tell about the hours I'd spent planting a bright flower garden and Erica would say, "My mom liked to dig in the dirt and get muddy," as if she were reporting on Gizmo, our family dog. The sacrifice of my walk-in closet would never come up.

I could just see the travesty they'd make out of my funeral. I'd better write it all up ahead of time, and tell them to stick to the script or forget it. Maybe I'd have Nick be the sole speaker, and leave everyone thinking I'd been the Mormon answer to Mother Teresa . . . only a tad more adventurous.

I pressed a cassette into the tape player. "Let's listen to some Beethoven," I said. (This effort to expose my children to great classics will also, undoubtedly, go unmentioned at their farewells.)

"Hey, I heard that music on Muppet Babies," Ryan said.

"I thought that was the tune on Mike Tyson's Punch Out." Grayson, the music lover.

These are the children who thought I was kidding when I explained that the Ninja Turtles were named after actual artists. They made me look it up in the encyclopedia to prove it.

"You're humming," Erica said. "You always do that when you're upset."

"Like when Uncle Nick is coming over," Grayson said.

Erica nodded. (Two detectives agreeing on the evidence.)

"Oh, go to school and have a nice day. I love you," I barked as I pulled up to the curb.

Grayson and Ryan piled out, then Erica turned her pitying eyes back to me. "The *flavor* of the ice cream was okay," she said. "It was just the texture that was funny."

"Thank you, sweetheart," I said, as she kissed me and waved good-bye. "You're a real pal."

CHAPTER 11

THE LEAP OF NO FAITH

I'd planned to stay home to supervise the workmen that day, but within an hour I got an emergency phone call from Shelby Verne, the wife of our elders quorum president.

"I was just visit-teaching Justine Overland, and I think you'd better go over there," Shelby said.

"Why—what's the matter?"

"Well, she was staggering around and her words were all . . . I don't know. And she kept dozing off."

I didn't ask any more questions. I just jumped into the van and sped over. It could be anything at all, from the visiting teacher's description. Justine was pretty young for a stroke, but you never know. And what if it were an overdose?

Justine and Steve had been in the ward such a short time. We'd visited her as a presidency. She seemed like a terrific girl. She even made regular visits to the welfare farm to pick fruit (with or without a decent map). Certainly nothing indicated a drug problem. Steve seemed to adore her.

"Justine?" I called through her door. "Are you in there?"

Justine staggered to the door and let me in. "Good night," she said as I walked in.

"Do you feel all right?"

"Sure . . . I just feel so tired." Her eyes were glassy.

"Justine, have you taken anything?"

"Sure, the pain killers I got from Steve's doctor. They're for my headaches."

"How many did you take?"

Justine was curling up on the sofa. "Just every four hours . . ."

"Do you have the doctor's phone number?"

Just then Steve came rushing through the door. "Darling, are you okay?" He looked terrified as he picked her up.

"Hi, honey," she mumbled.

Now Steve turned to me. "Shelby called me at work, so of course I'll take care of her now. Thanks for everything."

Steve began heading out the door. "Do you know where the closest emergency room is?"

"Follow me," I said.

We had a better turn-out at the hospital than we get at some ward picnics. The bishop, his counselors, the mission leader—it seemed half the Primary board was there, too. Lara carried a huge bouquet, quickly picked from her garden, yet arranged perfectly by Lara's artful hands.

Cam Verne, the elders quorum president, followed behind with Shelby, who must have an automatic dialer on her telephone.

"I'll bet they have to pump her stomach," Shelby whispered to me as she breezed by.

Sure enough, Justine seemed to have taken too many pain pills. Several of us waited in the hall until Justine felt well enough to have visitors.

"Psst! Steve, can I talk to you?" Cam motioned Steve a few feet away, where I overheard him say, "Listen, how well do you really know Justine? I mean, I know you guys got married pretty fast after you met—"

"What do you mean?" Steve asked.

"I don't know . . . some pain killers are pretty addictive," Cam said in grave tones. "I'd keep a close eye on her."

Steve patted Cam's arm. "Thanks for your concern," he said. But from the way he said it, you knew any further concern which implied Justine was a drug addict would not be welcome.

Steve went in alone to Justine, then headed down to the gift shop to get her a "pick-me-up."

"Did you hear that?" Shelby whispered to me. "I'll bet Steve's behind this whole thing, and he's gone out to get her more drugs."

"What?" I couldn't believe my ears. Then Shelby, Phoebe, and several of the other women dashed into Justine's room. I followed them in.

"Listen, Justine," Shelby said, in a you-can-tell-me tone, "how well do you really know Steve?"

"Huh?" Shelby was clear-headed now, but understandably puzzled by Shelby's question.

"I mean, he's the one who gave you the pills, right?"

"Yes."

Shelby tilted her head to one side. "Well, I'd certainly keep an eye on him." I interrupted with what I hoped were statements slightly more comforting than Shelby's (not tough to do), but soon Shelby was rescuing Justine again.

"Listen, if you feel unsafe or you just want some time to think over this new marriage, you can stay with me," Shelby said.

"Oh, it's not like that," Justine insisted.

Shelby glanced at the rest of us. "She could be enabling him," she said. "Or afraid. What she really needs is to get away and think this thing through."

I rolled my eyes. "Shelby, can I talk with you for a minute?" Out in the hall, I asked her how she was so certain that Steve was the culprit here.

"Haven't you seen how he dotes on her?" Shelby said. "He is so controlling, Andy. It's all because he's got her hooked on drugs! Weren't you suspicious when he came home so fast and said he didn't need anyone's help? He wasn't even surprised that she had overdosed!"

"But, Shelby, this is quite a serious accusation—"

"What if I'm right and nobody helps her get out of there? I mean, they hardly know each other! He probably laced her orange juice with something."

I laughed. "Laced! You sound like a mystery writer."

"Well, he could have done exactly that!" Shelby had her hands on her hips; her chin jutted defiantly into the air. "Also, why didn't she get the prescription from her own doctor, instead of Steve's? Don't you think that's weird?"

"Not really. When they married, she just automatically went to Steve's doctor. She's from Hollywood, so—"

"Aha—she's from Hollywood. What does that tell you?"

"It tells me she's from Hollywood, Shelby. You're jumping to a lot of conclusions."

"Why didn't she say *our* doctor? I'll bet Steve and the doctor are both in on this."

Just then Steve rounded the corner with a floral arrangement, circling wide around Cam, lest he be cornered again with more advice. When he went in to see Justine, he asked if they could be alone.

"See?" Shelby whispered. "That's *weird*."

"To want to be alone with your wife?" I hissed. "And the drugs you thought he was getting turned out to be flowers."

Shelby snorted. "You think he's going to carry a bag of drugs out in front of him? They're hidden in the flowers!"

"You need a doctor worse than Justine does," I said. "This is really unfair."

Just then we heard gales of laughter coming from Justine's room. Shelby nudged me and raised her eyebrows, as if we now had proof that drugs were being used.

"Andy," Justine called, "Come and hear this."

Steve was wiping his eyes, still cracking up when I walked in. "You tell her," he said to Justine.

She stopped laughing enough to talk. "Steve was just telling me that Cam Verne was worried for him because he hasn't known me very long, and Cam thinks I'm a drug addict. Then I told Steve that Shelby had just said the same thing. Only she's worried that I haven't known Steve very long and *he's* the one pushing the drugs."

I laughed. "I think the problem here is definitely one of too little knowledge, but not on your part." I glanced toward the hall. "Looks like some people jumped to some pretty crazy conclusions."

"You know, those pills made me so drowsy that I couldn't remember if I had taken one," Justine said. "So I would take another one. And then in an hour or so, I couldn't remember . . ."

Steve kissed the top of her head. "No more pills for you," he said. "You scared me to death." I watched how dearly he loved Justine and marveled that anyone could find it suspicious.

"Sometimes the best help we can give is just to get out of the way," I said. "I'm so sorry." The two of them started chuckling again. "Sometimes this ward is a little *too* friendly," I said, trying to explain the extreme interest everyone had taken in them. "I'll go tell everybody to button it and go home." Then I went out into the hall and did just that.

"But Shelby," Steve said, suddenly appearing in the doorway, "thanks for dropping by when you did. You really saved Justine."

Shelby turned around and grinned. This was the very comment she'd been waiting for. "Thank you," she smiled, then said no more.

CHAPTER 12

THE KNOTS IN THE FAMILY TREE

What can you say about a meatloaf that died? That it wasn't beautiful, nor brilliant. That it loved neither Mozart nor Bach nor the Beatles nor me. It simply sat there like a chunk of asphalt, overcooked by at least an hour.

I'd been detained at two homes where I needed to fill out welfare forms. While I was glad to help those members get the food and supplies they needed from the bishop's storehouse, I knew I'd have to serve petrified meat to my own family that night. Someday a genius is going to invent a remote control oven, and every Mormon woman on the earth will buy one.

That evening, as we chiseled at our late dinner, Grayson asked if we could watch one of the kids' animated videos, *The Land Before Time*, for family home evening. "There's a good lesson in it," he added quickly.

"What lesson?" Brian asked.

"That you should stay together as a family."

"Grayson," Erica said, as patronizingly as possible, "there's a giant earthquake in that movie, and it splits the families *up*."

"Right," Grayson said, "but the boy dinosaur should have stayed with his mother. Because, even though she was dead, he could have used her for cover." And there it was: the definition of a mother's worth, out of the mouth of my babe. Those mission farewells were really going to be something.

Brian was chuckling and glancing my way to see if I was enjoying this new dimension to my value. Then he turned to the kids. "How about faith, obedience, and searching for our ancestors? Aren't those some good lessons from that movie?"

"Yes, yes!" The kids weren't even listening; they were just cheering their votes for a family home evening of popcorn and television.

"Since when are you an expert on kids' videos?" I asked Brian.

"Oh, I love that one," he replied. "You know—with Ducky and Littlefoot?"

My husband, the movie critic.

"Fine," I said, glancing up at our family home evening chart. "I see Grayson just filled his lesson assignment with the help of modern technology. Erica, it's your turn to provide the music. Do you have some prehistoric hymn we can sing?"

"How about Rock of Ages?"

"Yes, yes!" Grayson and Ryan, mouths full, screamed their approval.

"It's not a rock song," I said.

Silence. "It's not?" Ryan asked.

"No. And I notice you're in charge of refreshments."

Ryan's eyes twinkled. "Do we have any chocolate pudding?" he whispered to me. Ryan likes everything to be a surprise. His kindergarten had made tar pits the month before by sticking dinosaur crackers into bowls of dark pudding, and he'd been dying to make them himself ever since. An evening with the Flintstones. I could hardly wait.

"Hey," Brian said, patting my bottom, "I liked the way you tied in dinner with the dinosaur theme. You know, fossilized meat loaf and all—"

I whipped around, clutching the spray nozzle from the sink. "Watch out—I've got a banana, and I'm not afraid to use it!"

"*Babar, The Movie*. Since when are *you* an expert on kids' videos?" Brian reached into the cookie jar.

"What's happening to us?" I asked him. "I actually

quote Mr. Rogers. I sit down to watch *The Little Mermaid*, the kids all run out of the room, and I still sit there, mesmerized."

"Me too. We must be good parents."

I laughed. "Right. I'm sure that's it."

Just then the doorbell rang. "It's Grandma Taylor!" Ryan, our lookout at the window, shouted.

"Ma, what are you doing here?" This is Brian's standard greeting to his mother. It is also the example our children will probably copy when I visit *them* someday, and it will no doubt help to explain the lack of appreciation which will be expressed at their mission farewells.

"Brian!" Both his mother and I expressed our dismay.

"Oh, come on," Brian said. "I'm happy to see you."

"Repeat after me," his mother said, her husky Eastern voice enunciating every syllable. "Ma, what a pleasant surprise."

Then Brian, doing a darned good impersonation of his own mother, said, "Ma, what a pleasant surprise."

Satisfied, Grandma Taylor breezed in and began talking. "This morning my friend Claire Evans—you remember her, the one who had her nose done—anyway, she said she had to visit her sister and asked if I wanted to ride along. So here I am! She'll be back to pick me up in the morning, if you don't mind having a houseguest overnight." The kids all cheered.

"Wonderful!" I said, taking her jacket.

Grandma Taylor glanced at the empty table. "Oh, good. I've missed dinner."

Tact runs in their family. "Pardon me?" I said, teasing.

"I mean, I wouldn't have wanted to impose."

She wouldn't have wanted the dinner, either, I thought to myself. "Can I fix you something?"

"Not a chance."

I raised my eyebrows, and she laughed. "That didn't come out right. What I meant is that Claire and I ate dinner just before we got into town. We stopped at the best place for liver and onions—"

"Yu-u-uck!" The children said in chorus.

"In that case, you're just in time for family home evening," I said.

"That's one of those Mormon deals, right?"

Brian laughed. "We knew you were coming, so we hurriedly planned this just to trap you and convert you, Ma."

She smiled, well accustomed to his ribbing. Brian had joined the Church in his teens, but was never able to get his parents to follow along.

"It's really fun," I said. "It's a time for closeness and communication. Usually we have a lesson or an activity—"

"And *always* we have refreshments," Erica chimed in.

"Tonight we're watching a video!" Ryan and Grayson pulled her to the sofa.

"Oh, sounds like lots of closeness and communication to me," Grandma said.

I smiled. Okay, so watching a video is not the way to get to know one's family. On the other hand, last week the kids had a major fight over the size of Noah's ark, so maybe a verbal discussion wouldn't be such a terrific missionary moment either.

"Why don't we watch the tape another night and visit with Grandma for family home evening?" I said in sweet tones, turning my back to her so that I could stare down my kids and let them know that there had better not be any groans about it.

"Can we still eat tar pits?" Ryan asked.

"Oh, I hope so," Grandma Taylor said, oozing insincerity.

Ryan laughed. "You'll like them, Grandma. I double promise it."

In no time the kids were so busy talking with their grandmother that they forgot all about the movie. Soon our spoons were clinking as we polished off Ryan's pudding in the dining room. We put the kids to bed, then sat down with some tall glasses of lemonade.

"I have a new neighbor," Grandma said. And then, as if revealing a choice tidbit, "I found out he's *Hawaiian* and he teaches *karate*. How about that?"

Brian and I gave the expected oohs and aahs. "It's probably Nick," Brian whispered.

"The retirement community's getting very exotic, I tell you," Grandma Taylor went on. "We had Cajun blackened steaks last week."

Brian whistled.

"Personally, I think the cook burned the meat, and then tried to say it was on purpose, you know. And last week—did I tell you?—Miriam Pinski got new reading glasses. You should see them—huge, violet frames. On a woman her age! She said a fashion coordinator told her she has the face for drama. Drama, can you believe? And violet, yet. Next week my neighbor is starting karate lessons for seniors."

"You signing up?" Brian teased.

"I'm a widow, for heaven's sake." Grandma sipped her lemonade. "You use fresh lemons in this? I can tell. You can always tell when they're fresh, you know? There's something different about it. Very good. And I hope you don't throw your lemon rinds away, dear. Put them down the disposal so it'll smell fresh. Oh, and before I forget—" she rummaged through her many-pocketed purse, then glanced toward the stairway before lowering her voice. "Here. I brought a birthday card for Grayson. I know he's turning eight next month."

"Oh, how sweet of you," I said.

"I didn't sign it. You know me, I never do. That way, you can use it again." Grandma Taylor beamed proudly.

"You certainly think of everything, Ma." Brian tucked the card away.

"So, Andy, are you still the president of the Relief Society? I don't know how you deal with all those women. Any of them have PMS? I couldn't put up with that for five minutes. That's one thing I like about the retirement village—nobody can get crabby and then blame it on PMS."

I laughed. "Actually, there are some sisters who really suffer terrible depression with it. My heart goes out to those women."

"Not mine," Grandma Taylor snapped. "Cheer up or go home and take a hormone pill, I always say. In all my days I can only think of one thing I've finally learned about women."

"What's that?" Brian asked.

Grandma leaned in. "That every woman thinks her own potato salad is superior to the potato salad of every other woman."

"Grandma Taylor, you are so right," I laughed. Despite her cynical, chatty style, I really love Brian's mom. I can't help thinking that if Nick were her son, she would never have disowned him, as my own mother did. She'd probably go right along with his eccentric stories, even topping them now and again.

"Tell me the truth, Alexandra." She enjoys rolling my full name over her tongue. "Wouldn't you say there are at least five or six women in your church who could benefit from just the right medication?"

I laughed. "What do you mean, Mom?"

"Well, I have a theory." She held up a petite little finger, bent with arthritis. "In any organization where you have a hundred women or so, there are always five or six who could use some time on the couch and a good prescription."

Brian and I cracked up. How did she know? I'm ashamed to admit that several names did come to mind, despite my efforts to resist compiling a mental list.

"Andy would never tell you, even if she agreed," Brian said.

His mom smiled. "I know. You can't criticize other people in the Mormon church."

I wished all the *members* thought that!

Grandma went on. "That's why you need *me* to do it for you. I'll start with Leonard Hickly."

"Who's Leonard Hickly?" Brian and I always manage to play right into her hands.

"I'm glad you asked." Then she went on to share all the local gossip from the retirement community, from Nyla Atkinson's Civil War locket that turned out to be a fake, to Leonard Hickly's cheating at bingo.

Brian smiled. "Why don't you stay the whole week, and we'll drive you home Sunday, after church."

"Oh, yes," I said. "We don't see enough of you. And the boys would love to give you their room. They think sleeping bags are a great adventure."

"No, you'll drag me to church again. And it will probably be Fast Sunday. I don't know how you do that either. I always fast better on a full stomach. Of course, I did like that lesson on honoring your parents last time I was here. That's always a favorite subject of mine." She glanced at Brian, smirking.

"Oh, boy, look at the time," Brian said, sensing a lecture fast approaching. "Gotta get up early for work and school."

"People should get up early *anyway*," Grandma said. "It's good for them."

The next morning, as usual, Grandma was first to rise and had devoured the newspaper by the time we all converged in the kitchen.

"Lakers blew it in overtime," she said, neatly folding the sports section.

Brian groaned. "How about a simple 'good morning,' Ma?"

"*And*," she said, ignoring him, "now they've lost the home court advantage."

Brian stood, just looking at his mother. "You do this on purpose, I know it."

"Do what?"

"You come into town whenever a critical game is being played so that you can be the first to bear bad tidings."

Grandma snickered.

Just then Grayson came around the corner, ready for school. "I heard Grandma singing 'Splish Splash I was taking a bath,' so I got up early."

Brian busted up laughing. "You were singing 'Splish Splash'? I can't believe it!"

"I *always* sing that in my morning shower," Grandma huffed. Then she turned to Grayson. "But I'm sorry I woke you, Dear."

"Oh, that's okay. Whenever we get ready for school early, Mom lets us play a game. Wanna play poker with me?"

I cringed.

"Where did you learn how to play poker?" Grandma

asked him.

"Mom taught me." Grandma's eyes grew round. Grayson went on. "We only have fish cards, but I can tell you what each thing stands for."

Grandma Taylor declined, saying she played plenty of cards at the retirement village. Then she turned to me. "Well, I see you're teaching my grandson the important things in life."

I could feel myself blushing. Okay, so I used to sit and play poker with the other little girls in my neighborhood. But we never bet or gambled. So when Grayson sprained his thumb at the bowling alley (another family home evening disaster) and couldn't bowl, the only video machine available for consolation was the poker one. So that Grayson wouldn't have a *completely* miserable evening, I dipped into my childhood memory banks and taught him the thrill of a royal flush.

Suddenly, I saw yet one more glimpse of Grayson's future mission farewell: "I'd like to thank my mom, the Relief Society president, for teaching me how to play poker. I know I'll use it in the mission field—"

"Grandma," Grayson said, "Are you coming to my baptism next month when I turn eight? Daddy's going to baptize and confirm me."

"Oh, I don't know, dear," Grandma said. "I'm on a pretty tight budget these days."

Grayson looked disappointed. "Well, I'll tell you about it after, then." Grandma Taylor kissed his cheek and Grayson asked, "Have you ever been baptized?"

"Yes, as a baby into some church or other. I forget which one it was."

"Have you been confirmed, too?"

Grandma Taylor winked. "Well, I've had my suspicions confirmed once or twice. How's that?"

Grayson laughed. "That's not the same, Grandma! This kind lets you belong to Christ's actual, same church that he made when he was here. And you get the gift of the Holy Ghost, too."

She gave him a hug. "I'm certainly proud of you, Grayson."

Just before it was time to take the kids to school, a horn beeped in the driveway and Grandma Taylor kissed everyone goodbye. Brian and I walked her outside. "You're a wonderful mother," she whispered to me as she left. "I'm so grateful Brian found you."

"I'm grateful too," I said. "And you're not such a bad mom yourself."

She cocked her perky gray head to one side and strutted down the walk. "Well," she said, as boastfully as possible, "some of us got it and some of us ain't." Then she threw us all a kiss as she rode away.

Brian and I stood at the curb, waving until the car disappeared.

"I really love your mom," I said.

"Quite a character," Brian added. "She just keeps getting snappier . . . and thriftier."

I knew Brian was hurt that his mother wouldn't be coming to Grayson's baptism. "She doesn't understand the importance of Grayson's baptism," I said, putting my arms around him.

Brian shrugged. "I guess."

"Speaking of birthdays, I'd better call my family about Nick's."

Brian smiled. "You never give up, do you?"

"He's my brother. I can't."

As we walked back into the house, Grayson said, "There's somebody on the phone named Shazam! And they want to talk to Mommy!"

I laughed and picked up the phone.

It was Zan. "Hi, Andy, it's Zan. I know Nick's birthday is coming up, and I wanted to get him something. Could you give me some ideas? I want it to be really special."

"Whew. Hmm. Let me see," I said, waving to Brian, "a good idea for a birthday gift for Nick."

Brian whispered, "How about one of those Monopoly 'get out of jail free' cards?"

"Well, unlike some men," I said, elbowing Brian, "Nick is pretty easy to buy for. I'm sure he'll like anything you choose." Brian's tastes were so precise that it was nearly impossible to buy gifts for him. It had to be just the certain fishing pole that he alone knew how to pick, or just the kind of shirt with a particular collar, or one special piece of stereo equipment that only his expert eye would recognize.

"I know Nick's very sentimental," Zan said. "He talks about his childhood so often, about how you practically raised him, Andy."

I felt warm all over to hear this compliment. Then a little fear gripped me. If my input turned out a guy like Nick, what would my own children become—gangsters?

"Hey, I know the perfect gift," I said. "How about transferring some old home movies to videotape for him? I have some footage of Nick as a little boy, riding his first pony, blowing out birthday candles, feeding a peanut to an elephant at the zoo, some track and field stuff—"

"Oh, I love it!" Zan was downright gleeful. "I knew you'd think of the perfect thing."

"Hey, that gives me a good idea, too," I said. "I know a way to transfer photos to fabric. I can transfer some old family photos onto quilt squares, then my sisters and I could tie him a memory quilt!"

Zan was almost giggly. "I love it! He'll be so surprised." Then she surprised me. "We're very much in love," she said.

Yikes! I felt icy heat envelope my entire head, frizzy hair included. "Yes, he seemed pretty smitten with you from the minute you met."

"Andy, I have never met a man like Nick before."

Has anyone?

"I mean," Zan continued, "this is going to sound egocentric, but other men have always been intimidated by me. But not Nick."

"Well, now that you mention it, I can't think of a time in Nick's life when he did feel intimidated."

"And I love that!" Zan sounded seventeen.

If it's overconfidence you like, I thought to myself, you've hit the jackpot.

"You know, Andy," Zan said in a serious tone, "I owe you an apology for something I said at that bridal shower."

"Gee, I thought *I* did most of the talking that night."

"No. It was when you won that game and you said the skills had come from mothering. Remember? I made a joke in poor taste, that people say motherhood has no rewards."

"Oh, Zan, I knew you were just teasing."

"But I felt so . . . jealous of you that night."

"Are you serious?" I had to sit down.

"There you were, happily married—I could tell—with children, and you seemed so content. I'm really ashamed that I put it all down. The real truth is, those are the things *I've* always wanted. I believe motherhood is where the real rewards are."

"Oh, Zan, no apology was needed. I'm flattered that someone of your stature would be jealous of *me*." I chuckled. "To be perfectly honest, I think you just made my day."

"Well, I didn't want you to think I had my priorities *completely* out of line. Nick and I have had some long discussions about priorities, honesty, and integrity."

Had I been sipping some orange juice, I would have choked.

Zan thanked me again for the gift idea, said good-bye, and then I drove the kids to school.

"If Uncle Nick marries that lady, we'll have an Aunt Shazam!" Ryan whispered to Erica. "I can't wait to tell Dakota." Dakota is the little boy in kindergarten whose claims rival even Nick's. Dakota insists that he found an actual buried treasure of gold coins last summer, that he personally brought a dead lizard back to life once (sign him up to teach Relief Society), that his dad holds a weight-lifting record, and that if you bury a walnut under your window, your house will turn into a rocket by morning.

Naturally, having a relative named after a genie would be a real coup for Ryan.

When I got home, I called my mother and sisters to see what they thought about making Nick a quilt.

"He'd probably sell it the minute he unwraps it," Mother said. Okay, one down and two to go.

"What's he going to do with it if they arrest him—

take it along to San Quentin?" asked Natalie, my youngest sister, who wouldn't have finished school if I hadn't lent her my entire collection of term reports.

"I'm not speaking to Nick," Paula said. Two years my junior, Paula has evidently forgotten the two million times she has said, "I owe you one," when I've rescued her from financial ruin.

"Boy, talk about family unity," I said. "Why can't you guys just bury the hatchet and forgive him? So he tells a few wild stories—"

"Nick gives me a pain," Paula said. "My analyst says the best thing to do with people like that is to cut them off."

"Oh, great advice, Paula." I can't believe she's still in therapy after eleven years (getting, I might add, rather questionable counsel). "I'm sure that's what the Savior meant in the Sermon on the Mount, when he—"

"Here we go again. The Relief Society president."

"Hey, what's the difference what calling I have? You don't just cut off a brother that you're sealed to in the temple. You try to forgive and love him."

"Just because you're older," Paula said, raising her voice, "you think you can tell the rest of us what to do."

"Paula, stop. Every year I ask you guys to help celebrate Nick's birthday, and every year you dig in your heels and refuse."

"For your information," Paula said, a line she has been using since nursery school, "I'm on the verge of a nervous breakdown."

Oh, boy, I thought. This again. "Hey. If anybody in this family is going to have a nervous breakdown, it's going to be *me*," I said. "I'm the one who's earned one!"

"Well, I just might have one," Paula said, as if looking over a menu and deciding whether or not to have a dessert. "My therapist said I should eliminate all stress from my life. I even quit my church calling."

"What?" (I'm all for explaining one's realistic limits to the bishop, but refusing to staple the ward newsletter on the advice of an uninspired quack—)

"It was just too much for me," Paula said. "We're not

supposed to run faster than we're able to. I know my scriptures well enough to remember that one."

Certain people should never read certain verses, you know? They twist them to suit their purposes, and then you can't pry them loose.

"Well, how about John 3:16?" I asked her. "For God so loved the world, that he gave his only begotten Son, that whosoever believeth in him should not perish, but have everlasting life."

"So?"

"So God did all that and you can't even give five minutes to the Church?"

With that, Paula hung up on me, an action that will probably thrill her therapist.

I sat and pondered my family's attitudes. I thought about my Relief Society job and the way we struggled and tried so hard to reunite families who had been torn apart by differences. How ironic that my own was in splinters. I thought about the founding of the Relief Society, and how it was always based on loving compassion, service to the community, relief of suffering, and a sisterhood that built testimonies of Christ. I thought about my chat with Claudia Lambert and how I'd told her some people simply *are* more easily overwhelmed than others.

Then I realized I'd been guilty of the very thing I had told Claudia was wrong—judging others' abilities to cope.

I called Paula back and got her machine. But I knew she was listening, so I went ahead and spoke. "Paula, sometimes I am really insensitive. I love you very much and I'd like you to forgive me. If you feel stressed out, I accept that. I guess I'm not practicing the gospel very well."

"Hi, I'm here." Her voice sounded tiny and hurt.

"Paula," I said, "I'm really sorry. Forgive me for thinking we're all just alike."

"Okay. But I still don't want to help with the quilt. It would just be too much for me."

"No problem," I told her.

Once again, I would do Nick's birthday myself—well, this time with the help of a magic genie.

CHAPTER 13

THE NOT-SO-FAST SUNDAY

"Where are the Hershey kisses?" I whispered to Brian.

He grunted.

"Wake up, Honey. I can't find the chocolates."

Brian opened his eyes and squinted. "I'll bet this is what it's like to be married to an alcoholic. They wake you up to ask where their stash is." He pulled the covers back over his head.

I pulled the covers down again. "Brian! They're not for me."

"Oh, ri-i-ight. It's Sunday morning and you're entertaining a house full of people."

"Come on. Help me look."

"I am not combing the house for Hershey kisses so that you can bribe the sisters to bring their scriptures every week."

I glanced at the clock. In one more minute I would be late to priesthood executive committee meeting. In our ward, Bishop Carlson likes to have the Relief Society president attend—on time if possible. Brian gets the kids ready while I'm in my meeting, then we all converge in the chapel for church.

But there was no more time to hunt for the bag of kisses. Every week we put a jar of 'scripture kisses' on the table, to reward those who bring their scriptures to church. Today we'd just have to skip it. Oh, well, it was Fast Sunday anyway.

I screeched into the parking lot just minutes ahead of a visiting high councilman. I missed the opening song, but by the time he joined our meeting, I appeared punctual and composed.

"How nice it is to see a Relief Society president at these meetings," Brother Hughes said. "And so prompt."

I blushed beneath the knowing stares of the other men in the room.

"You are so lucky," hissed Cam Verne. I grinned.

"How are the home teaching reports?" Bishop Carlson asked.

"Down four percent from last month," said the high priest group leader. "We missed quite a few families."

"Elders quorum?"

Cam fidgeted. "I don't know what to do with these guys. I get on them, but—"

Bishop Carlson just waited. Cam sighed. "Sixty-one percent," he said.

"And Relief Society?"

I tried to smile modestly and cleared my throat. "A hundred percent," I said.

Every head in the room whipped around to stare at me. Each week I stumbled in without a clue, unable to get information out of our supervisors. Our statistics were pretty good by the end of the month, but we'd never had a hundred percent before. And now that a stake visitor was here, we looked like we were running the tightest ship in town. I almost giggled.

"Well!" Brother Hughes said. "That is impressive." He leaned forward to look at me, leaned back, then leaned forward again. "I do believe you're the first in the stake to do that. Bishop, I'd recommend a promotion for this young lady, but I don't know what you could promote her to."

The other men gave him courtesy chuckles, but continued to stare at me, unbelieving. For them, I'm sure it was like watching the worst kid in your grade get a commendation from the principal.

"Maybe we'll just give her a raise," quipped Bishop Carlson. "Good job, Andy. Tell the sisters we're proud of them."

I blushed. Bishop Carlson then went on with other business, but the men in the room kept stealing incredulous glances at me, occasionally shaking their heads. I could almost read their thoughts: "What a break, to get a hundred percent the day the stake visits."

Cam was rolling his eyes, ready to gag. "You are so *lucky*," he whispered again.

I shrugged and smiled. At last! Something finally went right. But, as with all lucky breaks, this one was short-lived.

The minute we adjourned and headed into the foyer, Sister Delaney came rushing through the front doors, loudly claiming that she hadn't been visit-taught in two months. I was stunned. I didn't need to glance at this morning's doubters to see the smug expressions on their faces. By the time I talked with her and found she was mistaken, everyone else was gone.

I should have known my triumph was too good to last. When Brian and the kids arrived, I sat down and leaned over to pick up one of Ryan's coloring books and hit my head on the bench in front of me. Then, instead of rushing to my rescue, Brian held his sides in hysterical laughter and could scarcely sing the opening hymn.

Sister Delgado, our organist, was on vacation and the substitute organist needed all the help he could get. With Brian laughing at my goose egg, it was hard to keep the kids from giggling at the organist's sour notes. "Hear that organist?" Brian finally asked the kids. They nodded. "Well, that's how *you're* going to sound if you don't practice!"

"You should be ashamed of yourself," I whispered to Brian.

"What?" he said, as if utterly innocent. "This is an object lesson."

"Yes, and I'm the one who objects."

"Oh, spoken by the object lesson expert." Brian was whispering in my ear. "How about the time Ryan busted up Erica's Barbie Dreamhouse and—"

"Shh!"

Brian leaned in, determined to finish. "And you told her it was symbolic of the need to prepare lest the destroyer come!"

"Shh!"

"Yeah, Mom," Erica whispered. "Like Barbie's going to have a seventy-two-hour emergency kit. Right."

"Shh!"

Now I could hear Grayson and Ryan arguing.

"Did not!"

"Did too!"

"Did not!"

"Psst! Hey, you two," I whispered. "Be quiet!"

"Grayson threw his prayer rock at me this morning," Ryan said.

"Did not! I was tossing it onto my bed and you walked in front of it."

"Both of you, be quiet or we'll have a talk in the hall," I said. The boys had painted little prayer rocks in Primary to place on their pillows to remind them to say their morning and evening prayers. How ironic that within a week these sweet little reminders had become missiles of sibling rivalry.

Next, Grayson folded the program into a paper airplane, zoomed it past my eyes, and caused me to blink suddenly. One of my contacts slid down under my eye. I then discovered that I had somehow caught my paperclip bracelets (made by my sons) on my sweater, and I couldn't unfold my arms to work on my contact lens.

While I was thus struggling to free myself from a homemade straitjacket that even Edith Horvitz would have been proud to own, Brian unfolded Grayson's airplane, glanced at the meeting's program and said, "Oh, are you speaking today?"

"What?" Who knows what level of panic made my eyelids blink then, because now *both* my lenses had slipped beneath my eyes. Brian was chuckling again. When you're married to Brian, every day is April Fools'.

Suddenly, the sacrament hymn was over, my arms were still trapped in crossed position, and the deacons were passing the sacrament. Sister Surle, who was to my left, stood to walk down the bench to bring me the bread. I couldn't undo my arms to take any, and being blind as a bat without my contacts, I couldn't even see Sister Surle's face to determine whether she realized my problem. Finally I heard a disgusted sigh, and noticed that she had put the tray on the bench beside me.

"Erica, would you please get that?" I whispered. Erica was embarrassed ("totally," I would hear later) but fed me a piece of bread anyway.

When the water came, I had finally freed my right hand and replaced my left lens so that when Sister Surle held out the tray, I could grasp for the handle. But with only one eye corrected, my depth perception was off. I found myself grasping at fuzzy images of tray handles in the air.

Again, Sister Surle sighed and set the tray on the bench. Finally I located the real handle and tried to think about the Savior, instead of my own humiliation. I was not terribly successful.

Brian went up on the stand and vigorously began to conduct the choir. One lone, off-key voice echoed far above the others. We all knew it was Sister Marusa.

"How come that one lady always screams?" Ryan asked.

She probably has teenagers, I thought to myself. "Shh . . . she doesn't know she's screaming," I said.

"How come you don't sing in the choir, Mommy?"

"Who would watch you during Daddy's choir rehearsals?"

"Oh, yeah."

And anyway, I thought (but did not mention), the last time I had sung in a ward choir, I was wearing a suit that snapped shut. When I took a big breath to sing, half the snaps burst open and I had fled from the building in red-faced humiliation. My kids did not need another "Mom-ism" to tell at their mission farewells.

Next, Bishop Carlson introduced a new missionary, Elder Limbini. "Elder *Linguini*?" Grayson said, about a million decibels louder than necessary. The whole congregation heard him, and every kid there burst out laughing. I decided to add the elder to my apology list.

When it came time to bear testimonies, Sister Delaney got up and made a big announcement: She had been visit taught last month, but it was by phone and *she* didn't think that should count. So, here we were, with a legitimate one hundred percent, and one sister making me look like a sandbagger.

After the meeting Bishop Carlson spoke with me. Kindly, he didn't mention Sister Delaney. "See if you can get some more sisters to help out at the bishop's storehouse," he said. "Tell them how fun it is."

"I already have 'shop 'til you drop' written on the sign-up. Maybe I should tell them that the bishop's storehouse is really a storehouse of extra bishops. Then they can shop for a new one if they're disgruntled or offended. Can't you just see it? A bunch of guys in white shirts, stacked up on the shelves, and all these grouchy members going by with their shopping carts?"

He laughed, then took note of my forehead. "That's quite a bump," Bishop Carlson said. "You run into something?"

"Yes. Trouble."

There was more to come. In Relief Society the lesson was on long-suffering. Whenever I hear a topic like this, I'm immediately chagrined as I realize how impatient I am. If I were the teacher, I'd have to start every lesson with a disclaimer about my not really being an expert on the subject. (Unless, of course, the subject were how to wring object lessons out of everyday occurrences for child rearing purposes.)

Eagerly, I settled back to hear some inspiration on the subject and found myself nervously listening to our newest teacher. Her basic theme was that she strongly disliked California and that living here, for her, constituted long-suffering. Her dream was to move back to Utah, where she had been much happier. She then derailed onto the subject of how to get your husband to think it's his idea to move. Her plan consisted of leaving Utah tourism brochures under glass tabletops and folding open the newspaper to Utah real estate advertisements.

Ah, mistress of subtlety, to be sure.

I was struck with three thoughts: One, I didn't like the labels she was giving California *or* Utah. Two, I opposed the idea that husbands were to be coyly manipulated and were so weak that wives must make them think it's their idea. And three, if this guy were such a dolt that he wouldn't know those brochures were placed there by his wife, my hunch was that she could sell her house, pack up her belongings (including one not-very-bright husband), and move to Utah without his ever realizing they had changed residences.

At last I had to raise my hand. As gently as I could, I shared my view that we truly could bloom anywhere we're planted. Furthermore, I suggested that husbands and wives talk openly about their frustrations and wishes, not resort to hints and ploys.

It was the first time I felt I'd had to more or less correct a teacher. But as president, I was responsible for those kinds of errors. What if the sisters there had thought marital scheming was endorsed by the Church?

The teacher took it extremely well and went on to give a fabulous lesson. The spirit seemed to flow into the room. Then, just when I thought everything was back on track again, she ran a filmstrip. This one, set to music, showed picture after picture of a man on crutches, making his way to church. Inch by inch he hobbled closer, until at last he was seated in the chapel. The last frame showed the jubilant peace he felt at having endured hardships to gain a noble reward. I knew the teacher was hoping that we all got the same message: Long-suffering pays off. "So," she said, "would anyone like to comment on what the filmstrip was saying?"

Sister Spinkel raised her hand. "That we should get a ride if we're crippled," she said, "or at least a wheelchair."

Several sisters tried to stifle their snickers, and the teacher's mouth twisted in an effort not to embarrass Sister Spinkel. "Y-y-yes . . ." she said. "What else?"

Lara jumped in with the right answer, lest matters get worse. But she only postoned the worsening of matters until testimony time.

Normally, Relief Society testimony meetings go fine, but this time Sister Appleton stood up and bore, as near as I could tell, a testimony about a tipped uterus. Spurred on by Sister Appleton, Sister Thurman stood up. Her testimony was about her recent hysterectomy, and how this was an example of true sacrifice. From the corner of my eye, I could see Monica's mouth hanging open. I stared determinedly into my lap so our eyes wouldn't meet. The last speaker was Shiela Neff, who bore a patriotic, if somewhat angry, testimony about the wonderful state of California, staring at the teacher the entire time she was speaking. I closed my eyes.

"What in the world happened today?" Monica whispered to me after the meeting.

I shook my head. "I have no idea. Maybe they didn't get all the asbestos out when they remodeled the building and it has seeped into everybody's brains." The kids came roaring in from Primary, this time with spring flowers they'd fashioned out of Kleenex. Oh good, I thought. Those don't look likely to become projectiles.

When we got home, Gizmo had thrown up all over the house. "I think I know what happened to your scripture kisses," Brian said, scooping up a paper towelful of chocolate and tiny bits of foil.

I sighed. Should've named that dog Hoover.

"Hey, what's this?" Grayson asked, reading a skinny slip of paper amid the ruin. "You will obey your mother?"

"Oh," I said. "I guess Gizmo got into the pantry. Those were the fortune cookie messages I was going to put in your lunches tomorrow."

"Pretty pathetic," Brian said.

"Hey, I'm a desperate mom. What can I say?" I grabbed some rags to help clean up. "Gizmo," I said, "you only *think* you had a rough morning."

CHAPTER 14

PUTTING THE FUN BACK INTO "FUN"ERAL

If you've never attended a funeral where the bishop impersonates the deceased, well, you simply need to move into my ward.

Sunday night Brother Skinner died at the age of eighty-seven. He'd lived a good life and looked forward to hitting the veil at full speed. Mel Skinner had always been a vigorous dynamo, and until recently, he was the unstoppable activities chairman.

His wife, Brenna, was a busy temple worker, always bustling about—the perfect match for Mel. Her reaction to his sudden death from a heart attack was most remarkable. Her eyes would shine—more with hope than tears—as she expressed eager anticipation of seeing Mel again on the other side. "He'll be so glad to get rid of that lousy arthritis," she said. "And just think, when I see him next, it'll be just like a free face-lift. I won't have any of these wrinkles!"

When people expressed surprise at how well she was taking it, Sister Skinner just squeezed their hands and said with perfect pioneer spirit, "But I know we'll be together again soon. Temple work has built my faith into a mountain."

And when long-time friends would cry, Sister Skinner would say, "The only time death should be sad is when someone dies unrepentant. When the righteous die, they've won the battle! It's a time to celebrate. That's what Mel would have wanted us to do."

So we expected an upbeat funeral, as funerals go. I mean, Mormon funerals are usually quite uplifting anyway (and yes, sometimes even funny), but we were not prepared for the service Brenna Skinner had cooked up with the bishop.

"I've been asked to reprise a role of a ward member I played four years ago at a ward gathering," Bishop Carlson began. (Mel, as activities chairman, had asked several ward members to do this for the entertainment after a ward dinner.) "He got such a kick out of my attempt to 'do' Mel Skinner that Brenna asked me to do it again."

Now the bishop knocked loudly on the podium and began talking in the fast, no-nonsense style Mel Skinner had. "Hello, Brother Smith? Hello? This is the home teacher from hell and I know you're in there."

Everyone roared. Mel was relentless about his home teaching. He went religiously to every family assigned him, not just once a month, but once a *week*. He'd stand on the porch for half an hour, banging on the door until the hesitant family finally let him in. (Mel was always assigned hesitant families.) His style was brusque, but his heart was so sincere that he reactivated many.

"And then there was the time Mel Skinner got lice," Bishop Carlson continued.

Several people gasped.

"True story," Bishop Carlson said. "Mel had just been assigned a family who thought we Mormons not only avoided liquor and tobacco, but also water. Needless to say, their house could have used the services of Brother Jaxon (an exterminator). They no longer live in the ward, by the way. Anyhow, Mel went over the very day they'd gotten word about their grandma dying and gave every one of them a big ol' Mel Skinner hug."

I remembered it well. That very morning, Monica, Lara, and I had just done the same thing as a presidency. After hearing they had lice, none of us could sleep soundly for days. All week we kept nervously asking each other if any of us had noticed any symptoms. The next Sunday Monica had to give a talk. Lara and I sat in the congregation and pretended to scratch our heads feverishly, just as a prank to rattle Monica. None of us actually got lice from it, but we still laugh. Evidently Mel Skinner had not been so lucky.

"Well," Bishop Carlson went on, "it wasn't long before Mel was *truly sharing* with those he home taught." Everyone laughed. "Years ago, Mel visited a sister who insisted on giving him some caramels she had just made. Mel said no, he really didn't care for any. But then she looked so disappointed and said she'd made them just for Mel. So he took a bite. And they pulled his dentures right out! Now that's what I call going the extra smile for your families."

Bishop Carlson was getting more laughs than a comedian. Brenna Skinner seemed to especially enjoy the loving way he shared her favorite funny anecdotes about her husband.

"But what I'll always remember about Mel," the bishop continued, "is how he would get everyone to participate. Not many people know the little town of Camp Crest where Mel grew up. But when Mel was just home from his mission, the town council asked him to organize a Fourth of July parade.

"He got every man, woman, and child to march with a band, ride a horse, sit on a float—you name it. On the big day of the parade, Mel was sure this would be the most successful parade Camp Crest had ever seen.

"Well, I have to tell you, they *still* haven't seen it. Because everyone was *in* it! Mel had literally put the entire town in the parade, so as it moved down the streets, there was nobody—nobody!—on the sidelines to watch." We all began to picture the empty storefronts and the crowded parade and started laughing again.

"Now you know there *is* such a thing as being too successful," Bishop Carlson said. "Some years later, Mel tried to make it up to the community by having something where the majority *could* watch—a giant festival in the local stadium. Many of you are familiar with our dance festivals where thousands of young people fill the Pasadena Rose Bowl in beautiful costumes. Well, Mel tried it with—" Bishop Carlson paused, then squeaked, "cars."

Bishop Carlson stood there, shaking his head as we all realized the chaos and collisions you'd have trying to choreograph dozens of cars on a football field. By this time we were laughing so hard we could scarcely hear Bishop Carlson say, "That's right about the time Mel decided to move here." Brenna was enjoying it more than anybody.

On and on he went, telling Mel Skinner stories, and I felt a profound sense of regret. Not regret that Mel had died (we were all sure he was happily turning things upside down on the other side), but regret that Mel wasn't with us for that moment to hear the laughs and love that seemed to float up to the ceiling and form a giant canopy above our heads—a shimmering tapestry of his life. Maybe he *was* there long enough to enjoy the kind of knee-slapping tribute he was given. Even with all the laughter, Bishop Carlson managed to maintain the religious feeling a funeral should have.

The next morning, Brian and I went to the temple. "Do you realize," Brian said as we pulled into the parking lot, "that this is the first time in about a week that I've seen you without a phone attached to your head?"

I laughed. "You can always tell former Relief Society presidents. They have cauliflower ears."

"And," Brian added, "high-mileage cars and a closet full of unfinished crafts." Then he hugged me as we walked to the front steps. "But I love you, Andy. I think you're doing a dynamite job. I hope you don't think I'm complaining."

I stopped and kissed him. "I don't know how I'd make it without you, Brian. Hey. And tell me if I'm getting too busy with it, okay?"

He smiled. "Oh, I will. I *have*."

"That's true, you have. Now that I think about it—"

"C'mon," he said, pulling me to the door. "Afterwards, I'll buy you lunch at the Moroni Grill." (Brian's nickname for the temple cafeteria.)

While at the temple, I thought about Sister Skinner's matter-of-fact acceptance of Mel's death, her unwavering optimism—even eagerness—about dying. Then I wondered, What will I do if I lose Brian someday? Could I accept it with that kind of faith? That "perfect brightness of hope"? I shuddered, unable to fathom her level of strength.

Then, with sudden clarity, it came to me: One purpose of the temple was to bring us into an understanding and acceptance of the *whole* plan of salvation, including death. Without death there would be no point to life. Our whole purpose is to endure well and come unto Christ, I thought. Then we can return to live with him again. There would be no returning without dying.

Somehow, Sister Skinner had embraced these truths, drawn immense comfort from them, and even celebrated her husband's victory in his earthly stewardship. Her goal now was simply to join him when the time came.

I glanced across the room at Brian and pictured us rushing into each other's arms once both our tests were over. And then, as if he read my mind, he caught my eye, and smiled.

CHAPTER 15

CROOK OF THE MONTH CLUB

I was standing in line at the supermarket, minding my own business, when the man ahead of me suddenly remembered another item he had to buy. "Oh—" he shouted, rushing off, "will you watch my cart for just a minute?"

"Sure," I said. Slowly the cashier finished up with her customer, and still the man had not returned. "Guess I'd better unload his cart," I said, wanting to keep things moving. I left my cart, moved up to his, and began placing his items on the conveyor belt. "I'm sure he'll be back by the time you ring everything up," I mumbled.

One by one, I awkwardly arranged his bottles of beer, cognac, and vermouth. Somehow it wasn't surprising that Bishop Carlson came by at exactly that moment. He opened his mouth to greet me, but then saw the booze and stammered.

"Hi, Bishop, can I buy you a beer?" I figured if he didn't know me and trust me by then, he never would.

"Getting your year's supply?" he asked.

Just then—thank goodness—the man came back and thanked me for unloading his groceries.

"Were you really worried?" I asked Bishop Carlson.

"Well, it gave me a start. Listen, I'm glad I caught you."

"You did not catch me," I said, just for the record.

He laughed. "No, I mean, I'm glad I ran into you. I need you to visit a new family that just moved in and

requested church welfare. The Galloway family. I stopped
by briefly. Maybe you could teach them a little about
housekeeping, too, if they seem receptive."

Immediately I pictured Claudia Lambert and her
rifle. "Oh dear," I said. "If they shoot me, will you promise
not to impersonate me at my funeral?"

He grinned. "I promise. But see what you can do." He
wrote the address on a slip of paper.

"What we really need," I said, "is a video like *Scared
Straight*,—only this one will be for sloppy housekeepers
and we'll call it *Scared Tidy*. That way I won't have to deal
with it."

He laughed, peered closely at my purchases just to
give me a hard time, then left.

In the parking lot I had just finished loading my
trunk when Rita Delaney walked by. "Sister Taylor," she
began. I looked up.

Just then, the man whose cart I had unloaded drove
by and stopped. Rolling his window down, he said, "Hey,
you were pretty good swinging that beer up on the counter. Here's my card if ever you need a job." As he peeled
out, I stared at his business card. "Jungle Jack's Exotic
Lounge." I forced a weak smile and wilted beneath Rita
Delaney's stare.

"I watched his cart," I mumbled. Of all people to
bump into, why Rita Delaney?

Still she said nothing. "Did you want to talk to me?"

"Oh, yes." Sister Delaney glanced once more in the
direction of Cognac the Barbarian, then said, "I've decided
to get a new roommate. So if you hear of any LDS women
who'd like to rent a room, let me know."

"Oh, okay. Sure." She gave me the details, and I told
her I'd announce it on Sunday.

That evening I paid a visit to the Galloways. Bishop
Carlson was right about their apartment. It made Claudia
Lambert look like "Homemaker of the Year." Sister
Galloway moved some ashtrays off the table and brushed
some crumbs onto the floor.

"You can fill out the forms here," she said. She
seemed to know all about this.

Just then a toddler cried in the next room, and Sister Galloway went after him. I glanced around as I waited. Despite the mess, they didn't seem to really be *living* here. It looked more like a temporary stop. Clothes were still in suitcases. There were paper plates and cups on the counters as if they were fixing meals in a motel room. The doorless cupboards were empty, the walls were bare, and there were no toys anywhere—strange for a family with a baby.

Soon Sister Galloway walked in again carrying a little boy with big green eyes and sandy hair. "This is James, our youngest. We named our kids Matthew, Mark, Luke and James—after the first four books in the New Testament."

I smiled. So this was James, the one who would have been named John if his parents had ever cracked open a Bible.

"Where are the others?" I asked.

"Oh, they're in school." She plopped little James down on the floor, gave him an empty envelope to play with, and sat down herself.

"Well, that's good that you could get them right into school," I said. "How old are they?"

"Matthew is ten, Mark is seven, and Luke's five."

I smiled. "Four boys—that must keep you busy."

Sister Galloway smiled. "Yep. Plus trying to find work. My husband's out looking for a job right this minute."

"When do your kids get home from school?"

"Oh, about four."

I looked at my watch. "It's after five," I said.

"Oh, they like to go home with their friends sometimes." James had thrown down the envelope and was now scribbling on the wall with a ballpoint pen.

"Do you want him to do that?" I asked.

Sister Galloway shrugged.

"Looks like your sons made friends quickly. I have a seven-year-old boy myself," I said.

She smiled and glanced at my notebook. "Shouldn't we fill out the form now? We're a family of six."

I took a deep breath. "I'll need to talk with the bishop first, Sister Galloway. I hope you'll understand."

"Sure, no problem." Suddenly her jittery impatience was covered with a mask of cordiality, and she waved genially as I left.

I called the bishop at his work and caught him just before he left for home. "For the first time, Bishop, I don't feel good about giving assistance to this family," I said. That night I dropped off a box of our own kids' baby toys we had stored so at least James wouldn't have to play with pens and envelopes. Sister Galloway answered the door again, but no sound of youngsters was inside the apartment. She gratefully accepted the box, then slammed the door.

When I got home, Bishop Carlson called to say he had gone by right after I'd called him and had learned that this woman was not really LDS. She must have heard about our welfare program and evidently had managed to finagle some assistance here and there. She was single, and James was actually a nephew, quickly borrowed from her sister for the purpose of misleading me. Had his mother not come by to pick him up exactly as the bishop was arriving, he might never have discovered the ploy. So the family of six turned out to be a fugitive of one.

"Bet you're sorry you took all those toys over," Erica said as she helped me make dinner.

"No," I said, "the baby is innocent. In fact, if his own family is anything like 'Sister Galloway,' he probably needs those things more than ever."

Erica smiled. "I'm so glad—" and I was sure she would say, "that you're my mom," but instead she said, "that you didn't take over any of *my* stuff."

"Just the Barbie Dreamhouse," I said.

"Mom!"

I smiled. "C'mon, you never play with it anymore anyway."

But she was gone. She raced to her room and returned just as quickly, holding her heart like a 1930s movie star. "Thank goodness!" she said. "I thought you were serious."

I chuckled. Erica's husband is going to have a field day someday putting one over on her. She falls for everything.

Brian walked in, swung Grayson and Ryan in a circle,

then threw his jacket over a chair. "Guess what? The Caldwells gave us their tile cutter! Can you believe it? Those cost a fortune! Jim Caldwell said they've done all the tiling they're ever going to do, so he gave me their cutter, just like that! He said it was the least he could do to repay us for the airline tickets we gave them last year."

We'd had some non-refundable tickets to New York for Brian's family reunion last June, but had to cancel when Brian got a severe ear infection and couldn't fly. It just happened that the Caldwells' daughter was graduating from Yale that same week. The Caldwells were feeling sad that they couldn't afford to attend. We thought it would be a terrific surprise to give our tickets to these wonderful neighbors.

"Oh."

"That's all you can say—'Oh?'" Brian was pacing with excitement. "Do you realize how much that will save us in our remodeling if I can do the tile work myself?"

I pretended to be totally serious. "Brian, how could you accept a favor from the Caldwells? How could you let things get even when there's a missionary fireside coming up in three weeks?"

Brian just looked at me. "Oh, I see. You figure the Caldwells will join the church because we gave them tickets to New York."

"How do you expect to succeed as a missionary without keeping people in your debt?" I asked him. "Why do you think it's more blessed to give than to receive? Because then, they owe you one." I smiled.

Brian was cracking up. "I've heard some pretty amazing misinterpretations of the scriptures in my time, but this one takes it. Kids, your mother needs an ice pack."

I was laughing too. Maybe I *did* need a vacation. "Okay, but you have to go over and invite them," I said.

Brian shook his head. "No way. This is *your* little project. I already did my part."

"By removing their obligation."

"Exactly. Now, if they come, it will be for the right reason." Brian stole a pinch of Erica's grated cheese.

"Hey," Erica said, "no snitching."

Brian circled around by the brownies I was frosting and scooped out a piece with a spoon. "It drives me crazy when you do that," I said.

"Hey," he said, his mouth full of chocolate, "don't blame me for something that's been happening for years." He poured himself a glass of milk, then whispered in my ear, "I can't believe you were actually sorry that we got a free tile cutter."

I pushed him away, teasing. "I just hate to ask people to come to those things. I'm such a . . ."

"Wuss." Brian grinned, pleased that he found exactly the right word.

I smirked. "The word is 'shy.'"

"Ha! You—shy?! You're the one who asked *me* to marry *you*!"

I sighed. "I meant with missionary work. And as for asking you to marry me, I only did it because I could see you'd never amount to *anything* if I didn't rescue—" Brian had me on the floor, tickling me. I shrieked and laughed, and the kids ignored us completely.

"Erica, make Daddy stop," I wheezed.

She stepped over us to open the fridge. "You guys are always underfoot in here," she said.

"You probably wrestled people into the church on your mission," I hissed at Brian, who still had me pinned.

"Well at least I didn't resort to using *guilt*," he sneered. And then in a high, whiney voice (supposedly mine), he said, "Now you'd better come to church because I brought you that pie, remember?"

Finally I pushed him away, still panting and laughing. "Oh, all right. I'll ask the Caldwells myself."

Brian helped me stand up, then brushed himself off. "Boy, the extremes you have to go through around here just to make a point." Then he kissed me.

"Yuck!" Ryan can always be counted on for his unedited opinion.

After dinner the phone rang. "It's Edith Horvitz," I whispered to Brian, covering the receiver. "She says her whole house collapsed!"

Brian shrugged. "Bound to happen sooner or later," he said.

"Brian!"

"Well, it was."

"Brian!" I uncovered the receiver. "Hold on a minute, Edith." Then I covered it again. "Brian, I've got to pick her up. She's at a pay phone."

Brian put the boys to bed (or to sleeping bag, in this case, so Edith could sleep in their room) and I dashed over to what was left of her house.

She was right. The entire structure had collapsed like a pile of toothpicks. "Can't figure why this happened," she said.

I helped her sort through the rubble. She insisted upon stuffing every crocheted item she could salvage into the back of my van. "I don't want some crook to steal any of this," she said.

You could search the world over and never find a burglar so desperate as to steal a crocheted salt shaker, but I didn't say anything. "It's lucky you weren't inside when it happened," I said.

"I have my church calling to thank for that," she said. "I was at the store buying hemorrhoid cream for home-making night."

I gasped. She couldn't be serious.

"You can put it on your face, you know," Edith said. "I was going to teach the sisters how to use it for a home facial," she went on. "Shrinks the tissue."

What does one say to this—Eureka? Thank heavens a news reporter wasn't here to capture Edith's idea on tape.

"Oh, Edith," I said, trying to find the words to tell her she'd finally gone too far.

"'Course you don't want to shrink it *too* much," she said. I pictured tarry little shrunken heads, lined up in some shack in New Guinea. Pasted to the shelf was a little sign: "New Guinea Fourth Ward."

"Maybe we'd better skip that one—I mean, in case someone shrinks their tissue too much," I said.

We waded out of the particle board particles, and I drove her to my house. "Hey, I have an idea," I said. "There's a sister in the ward who's looking for a roommate.

Would you like to call her?"

"That would be wonderful," Edith said. It was remarkable how evenly she was accepting the demolition of her home. It was as if she were detached from the crisis somehow. Maybe *I* could use some of Edith's medication.

Soon Edith was chatting (and laughing!) with Rita Delaney on the phone. That very night she moved in with her.

"I'm so glad to have someone new," Sister Delaney whispered to me as Edith unloaded her things into her new bedroom. "That last roommate was just too unstable."

I forced a smile. Wait until you get to know Edith, I thought to myself. I considered speaking up, but then I thought, why not see how it goes? Obviously they've hit it off so far. And Edith *was* on medication that seemed to be helping. She was even starting to come out to church. So maybe this would be a good arrangement all the way around.

"I can't believe you did that to Sister Delaney," Brian said when I got home.

"What are you talking about? She asked me at the supermarket to help her find a new roommate."

Brian shook his head. "Edith is not a new roommate. Edith is a new dimension." Brian tossed a package of popcorn into the microwave and turned the dial. The oven began humming.

"Hey, she talked to Edith on the phone herself," I said. "She made her own decision."

"At last you're getting revenge on Rita Delaney."

"Brian Taylor, I'm shocked. Accusing me of getting revenge, when this whole thing just . . . happened."

"Just happened."

"That's right. Rita *just happened* to mention she needed a new roommate. And Edith's house *just happened* to fall down." I tried so hard not to laugh, honest I did, but suddenly I felt an uncontrollable giggling rising up through my chest.

"See?" Brian said. "I knew you were getting enjoyment out of inflicting Edith Horvitz on Rita Delaney."

"That's not it. I promise," I said, wiping my eyes. "Oh, Brian, I feel so bad to be laughing at such a terrible time.

Poor Edith." Then I started giggling again. "Brian, you should have seen that house!"

He just kept staring at me. "You're finally cracking up. And you should be worrying about poor Sister Delaney. She's going to be furious with you when she finds out what Edith is like."

I smiled, imagining it for a minute.

"See? You're enjoying this." Brian got a popcorn bowl out of the cupboard. The kernels were crackling and popping as the paper bag swelled inside the oven.

Finally I took a deep breath and stopped laughing. "Hey, wait a second. I'll bet it works out great. I'll bet Edith is the best thing ever to happen to Sister Delaney. And you know what? Nothing ruffles Edith. I'll bet if anyone could get along with Sister Delaney, it would be Edith Horvitz. And Edith really is kind of fun to be around, Brian. I mean, I've gotten to know her, now, and— I kind of like her."

Brian stared at me. "You really do like Edith, don't you?"

I surprised even myself. "I guess I really do! Yeah, I do. How come I always like the square pegs best?"

Brian shrugged. "You adore Nick."

I smiled, thinking about my little brother, imagining his face when he opened his birthday quilt next week.

As if reading my thoughts, Brian said, "He's gonna go nuts over that quilt you've been working on. And that videotape from Zan." The microwave beeped and Brian opened the door.

"That *was* a good idea, huh?" I said.

"Making popcorn?" Brian carefully tore open the steaming sack and poured the fluffy popcorn into the bowl.

"No," I said, "my stroke of genius in giving Nick a family memorial kind of birthday."

"You make it sound like a graveside service." Brian held out the popcorn and I scooped up a handful. "How come everyone in your family compliments themselves?"

I laughed. "I thought only Nick did that. Well, and my sisters and my mom, I guess."

Brian shook his head, chuckling. "All of you."

I blushed. Then I thought, why shouldn't we? "I think we're just . . . confident," I said. "And it *was* a good idea. Like that idea I gave you yesterday about your diet." Brian had been saying he needed some way to keep from snacking, and I suggested he write a list every morning of the foods he could eat that day—you know, a nutritious mix. Then he could cross each thing off as he ate it. But he couldn't eat anything that wasn't on the list. He loved the idea immediately and called it "The Andy Diet."

"That really was a good idea," he said.

"Hey, maybe I could get booked on talk shows. Before you know it, I'd have a national TV show of my own and I could teach people how to lose weight—"

"You missed your calling," Brian said. "You should have been a televangelist, or a radio psychologist. You and Nick. The Advice Family."

I laughed. "Just think. If I'd been born in India, I could be sitting cross-legged under a tree right now, wearing a batik-dyed skirt—the local wise woman."

"Oh, please . . ." Brian was rolling his eyes.

"People would line up for miles, just to ask me for dieting tips."

"Yeah, they need that in India right now."

I scoffed. "Well, they'd ask me for birthday gift ideas, then. I'd have a regular following. They'd call me Mahatma Andy."

"More like Maha-ha Andy. I can see it now," Brian said. "India's first comedy club."

I threw a kernel of popcorn at him. "A wise woman is never appreciated in her own house. Something like that."

"Especially when she's so stingy with her popcorn that she'll only throw one kernel at a time."

Just then the phone rang. I pulled a face at Brian and picked up the phone. It was Bishop Carlson.

"Well," he said, "thought you might like an update on Miss Galloway. Her sister has turned her in on welfare fraud. Looks like she's been bilking the state as well."

"Wow!"

"And guess what else? The sister wants to take the missionary lessons. Seems she was looking through a toy box someone gave to James this evening and ran across a Book of Mormon. How about that?"

How about that, indeed. Looks like the wuss approach isn't so bad after all.

CHAPTER 16

MARIMBA WARS

I know that we Church members don't believe in burly, neckless cave men who clubbed their women over the heads and dragged them across the tundra by their hair. But *if we did*, Elroy Morgenstrom would be the perfect specimen.

Grandma Taylor saw him at church last year, and said, "That man is a walking cure for agoraphobia. Rent him out! You send him into somebody's home with that raccoon coat of his and I guarantee they'll be outta there in five minutes."

Naturally, we were all surprised when Elroy decided to play tinkly little xylophone water glasses for the ward talent show Friday night.

He insisted upon being first up because he had such a delicate assortment of cups and goblets to arrange. When the curtains opened, a stage hand was just pouring the last drops of water into a crystal vase. Soon after, Elroy entered. His heavy steps jiggled the water in the glasses. He paused for a moment behind the table, then, clenching a spoon in each fist, began to play.

Boom, bang, smash, crash! Elroy struck the goblets so hard, it sounded like they were breaking. Suddenly water was splashing to the floor and we realized the cups *were* breaking—into a million bits. Chips of glass were flying into the front row, scattering the audience. Of course, my kids were cheering. "Hush!" I whispered, "Someone could get hurt!" They clapped and whistled all the louder. Brian had a distant smile on his face. "Where else but in this ward?" he muttered. "Once again it was inspiration to choose the back row." The year before we had sat on the back row and avoided getting splashed by Tempra paint as Dicky Peterson fashioned a wild watercolor for his talent. His easel had gone flying, cracking Brother Burnfield over the head.

I leaped from my chair to unlock the broom closet and begin sweeping up, but some men were already pushing brooms across the stage, trying to get things cleared for the next act.

Brian pulled me back down into my seat. "Look," he said, "it's just like the beginning of "Rocky and Bull-winkle," where they throw those flower petals and then it all gets swept up."

I sighed. What on earth possessed Elroy Morgen-strom to smash his glasses to smithereens? Then suddenly Elroy was at the mike saying, "Gosh, I guess you hit 'em a lot harder when you're nervous."

"I guess so," I said to Brian.

"Anyway," he said, "the song was supposed to be 'I'm a Little Teapot,' for those who couldn't make out the tune."

"The day Elroy Morgenstrom is a little teapot . . ." Brian muttered.

"Look!" I whispered, pointing to a young woman sweeping the stage, "Marla Verdugo is on the cleanup committee!"

Brian looked at Marla, then back at me. "So?"

"Well," I continued, smiling as I remembered packing her dishes for her, "I just think that's nice, that's all."

Brian shook his head. "You'll like the next number." He pointed to the printed program. "Edith Horvitz re-enacts the collapse of her house."

I snatched the program. "Let me see that." I scanned the lineup. "Oh, it doesn't say anything of the sort, Brian. It says she'll be doing a Carmen Miranda impersonation." I nudged him. "You're such a tease."

Then I gasped. *Edith Horvitz is doing Carmen Miranda?* "Oh, my goodness," I whispered.

And then the music began. Out danced Edith Horvitz

in a bright dress and a hat made entirely of crocheted fruit—crocheted bananas, crocheted grapes, and even a crocheted pineapple.

"Now I've seen it all," Brian said.

Just then Rita Delaney walked on stage, similarly attired, with a giant conga drum slung around her neck. "No," I said, "*Now* you've seen it all."

Brian's mouth was hanging open. Edith twirled and twisted to the music while Rita, her lips pinched as usual, kept perfect rhythm on her drum. They looked like two spinster sisters who'd known each other all their lives and had worked up a campy act for a family reunion. "I *told* you they'd hit it off," I said to Brian.

The music ended to the roar of applause. Edith and Rita took two bows. "Thank you," Edith said into the mike. "And I'd like to thank Andy Taylor for helping me find such a great roommate," she said.

"Hey—she's giving you the credit," Brian whispered. "Maybe you can become a talent agent in India."

"Shh!" I said.

"I feel I must have known Rita Delaney in the pre-existence," Edith went on.

"That's probably what pushed Edith over the brink," Brian whispered.

"Hush! I'm not going to sit by you if you keep making these comments."

"You and Daddy are disrupting the program," Erica said. "*Again.*"

"Sorry, Mom," Brian said to her.

Edith and Rita then took one more bow, and waved as they walked off stage.

Next, two little girls did a tap number, a quartet sang a couple of songs, and a deacon told some jokes.

"Time for *Marimba Wars*," Brian said, slouching down in his seat. Every year a pocket of tension swells up in the ward choir, making it hard for Brian to get the singers to rehearse. He has finally traced the trouble to the fact that his two best singers are both, as luck would have it, Marimba players.

"What are the odds," he once said, "of finding even

one Marimba player in the entire region? And we have two in one ward!" Naturally, because it would be too simple otherwise, they are bitter competitors, each trying to outshine the other on our yearly talent night. They've fumed over who goes first, who plays the longest piece, and who gets the most party and wedding reception bookings afterward.

"For Erica's reception we're having one guy with a tambourine," Brian said. "And he can hit it one time, then that's it. Bing. Done. That way nobody's feelings will get hurt."

"Except Erica's," I pointed out.

Brian shrugged. "She'll understand."

The first Marimba player pushed his instrument onto the stage. It was bigger than a xylophone and it took a couple of strong men to move it. He then began to play an elaborate Latin number that went on for eight minutes. Brian timed it by the number of times Ryan asked when it would be over.

After much grunting and groaning, his instrument was moved off the stage. Then, one exactly like it, possessing differences known only to the player, was painstakingly pushed into position. Then the second Marimba player entered. He was wearing an elaborate Latin costume, complete with a red satin sash and embroidered jacket. You could hear the audible gasp in the audience as we all realized that player number two had just edged out the competition in the costume department. We all knew the first player was probably fuming.

After eight *and a half* minutes, the second fellow finished his number. "Finally!" Grayson said, a little too loudly, and everyone laughed.

I slid down in my seat.

"Well, look at it this way," Brian said, "Maybe the guys will get the message and shorten their pieces for next year."

No such luck, I thought to myself. We both knew that next year the pieces would stretch to nine and ten minutes, and Player Number One would undoubtedly borrow Edith Horvitz's banana hat.

Next up in the talent show, was a high priest who played the spoons, followed by Grayson and Ryan as a ventriloquist and his dummy, respectively. The boys looked adorable (of course) but, unfortunately, they forgot to announce that Grayson was trying to be a ventriloquist. Their cute little conversation ended up looking like, well, just a cute little conversation between two brothers, one of whom prefers to sit on the other's lap.

"Oh, well," I said to Brian. We clapped wildly anyway.

Next, Erica and Kayla stole the show by lip-syncing and doing gymnastics at the same time. (As a mother I can be as biased as I want.)

And then it was time for Lara, Monica, Phoebe, and me. A month before, the activities chairman had asked the Relief Society presidency to do an act of some sort, so we put our heads together and came up with—nothing. None of us were entertainers, unless you count entertaining guests at a backyard cookout. Then Brian suggested we take the song, "If I Were a Rich Man" from *Fiddler on the Roof*, and rewrite the lyrics to say, "If I Were the Bishop."

Needless to say, we had the time of our lives dreaming up all the changes we'd make, and fitting them into the melody. We sang about reclining chairs in the Relief Society room, one big budget just going up, giving chocolates to all who visit teach, using fifty dollar bills for bookmarks, importing chefs from Paris to cook our meals, being driven to church in limousines. We even sang about putting Mr. Rogers to work in the nursery. Just before the last chorus, we turned our backs, stuck on mustaches exactly like Bishop Carlson's, tucked roses into our lapels (exactly like he wore each Sunday), then turned around and belted, "If I were the bi-shop! Daidle, deedle, daidle, digguh, digguh, deedle, daidle dum! "

We raised our hands and twirled around, kept on singing and had a heck of a good time. "Wouldn't it be nice for just awhile? Think of all the women who would smile. Wouldn't it be a lovely little trick—if I were in the bishopric?" Everyone was laughing, especially Bishop Carlson.

Then Chuck Mavis, the master of ceremonies, announced, "That's the Relief Society's version of 'To Dream the Impossible Dream.'"

Oh, well. Can't blame us for trying.

HEROES AND MIRACLES

You know your poor housekeeping has passed all sensible limits when a burglar trips over your stuff and breaks his leg.

And you can quote me, because that's exactly what happened to Claudia Lambert the night of the talent show. I'll explain.

After the talent show we all got home reasonably early. To my surprise, Jorja Willis—the sister who lost her grandchildren—was just coming down my front steps. "I rang the bell," she said, "but I figured you weren't home."

"Sister Willis!" I exclaimed, giving her a big hug. "It's wonderful to see you."

"I got your lovely note," she said, "and I'm sorry I slammed the door on you. I . . . can we go inside and talk?"

I seated her on the sofa, poured her a glass of ice water, and sat down beside her to listen.

"You said something that struck such a chord in me," she said. "I knew you were right and I was so ashamed of myself for not being more forgiving. Andy, I've been eating myself up with hate and resentment all these years. When you spoke to me on the porch that day, I just couldn't face the truth."

"You've been through a lot, Sister Willis."

"But I'm strong, Andy. What you said was true. I've always known it. And I *am* up to this challenge. You made me realize that my job now is to help others because of what I've been through. Someday somebody *might* need to lean on me."

I squeezed her hand.

She went on. "I must forgive Lorene Hausman, and my son as well. I must truly believe that God loves them, and that someday I will have a chance to know my grand-children."

"Sister Willis, this is the most wonderful thing you could tell me."

Tears of joy spilled out of Jorja's eyes, and she hugged me. "You woke me up, Andy."

"I just stood on your doorstep, Sister Willis. The Spirit of the Lord is what woke you up. I'm just glad we were both in tune that day." Then I began to cry, too.

Just then the phone rang. It was Claudia Lambert and she was hysterical. "I called the police to come and get him," she said.

"Get who?"

"The burglar. He fell over my things and can't move. I ran out of the house to a neighbor's. Kirk's out of town. Andy, what do I do?"

"Stay at the neighbor's until the police come," I said.

"I'm so scared. Please come over, Andy."

What am I, nuts? Go over to Claudia's neighbor's just to comfort a hysterical member when some deranged burglar could come springing through the window at any moment ? "I'll be right there," I said.

Then, just as I hung up the phone, it rang again. "Andy, it's Lorene Hausman. My date . . ." she started to cry. ". . . just beat me up. I think I'm hurt pretty bad. Could you take me to the hospital?"

I gasped. "Oh, Lorene!" I glanced back at Jorja, who turned white at the mention of Lorene. "Have you called an ambulance?"

"I can't—I don't have insurance."

I took a deep breath and tried to think. "I'll be right there," I said. Lorene could have critical injuries, while at least Claudia was safe at a neighbor's. I'd pick up Lorene, then call someone else from the hospital to go over to Claudia's. But who else knew her? Brian had to stay with the kids. I'd call Lara. No—I knew Lara wasn't home.

I looked up at Jorja. "Sister Willis," I said, praying for

inspiration, "could you take Lorene Hausman to the hospital?"

"What?" Her voice was barely a whisper.

"Please—it's an emergency," I said.

Sister Willis stared at me. This was the hardest question she'd ever been asked.

Finally, she nodded. I called to Brian, assured him I would keep my distance until I saw the police apprehending someone, then drove over to Claudia's neighbor's.

Two squad cars were already there, and a gurney bearing a man in dark clothing was already being loaded from Claudia's house into an ambulance.

"Looks like somebody knows martial arts," a medic was saying.

Well, I thought, if you can't personally do the guy in, at least scatter your appliances on the floor so he trips over them.

"They need me to come to the police station and file a report," Claudia said. And then in the euphoric tones that always follow a crisis, "I guess the guy broke his leg."

"Well," I said, giving her a hug and trying to elicit a smile or a sigh of relief, "serves him right. Maybe they'll give you a medal." I didn't think it would be the Good Housekeeping Seal, but perhaps Most Ingenious Booby Trap.

She laughed. "If they do, I'll come to church waving it in everyone's face."

I laughed, and gave her one more hug. "I'm so glad you're safe," I said.

She shrugged. "Sure. I know where all the stuff is!"

I shook my head, chuckling, as she drove away. Claudia Lambert, community hero.

From there I headed straight to the hospital. Lorene was being sewn up in the emergency room. They wouldn't let me in to see her. Eventually, Jorja came through the doors, pushing Lorene in a wheelchair.

"They say I can go home," Lorene said. "Nothing was broken." Her face was bruised and swollen, and she had a bandage on her forehead.

I put my arms around her. "Oh, Lorene. What a

nightmare you've been through."

As I pulled away, Jorja stroked Lorene's hair. "She'll be all right," Jorja said. Lorene began to cry. "Sister Willis, I can't thank you enough."

"Well, I was at Andy's when you called—"

"No." Lorene paused, choking back the tears. "I mean, for forgiving me. I never thought you would. I—" then she cried again for several minutes.

I looked up at Jorja's face and saw tears in her eyes. Jorja had found peace. She had finally relinquished the anger, and had passed the ultimate test: to truly love an enemy.

Lorene touched her bandage. "I don't know why I went out with such a jerk," she said. "I will never get over this. You can't trust anybody."

I patted Lorene's shoulder, then looked at Jorja.

Jorja knelt down beside Lorene, took her hand, and said, "Yes you can, Lorene. Right now you're angry, and you have every right to be. But you *can* overcome this. And I'm going to help you."

I stood on the curb, watching Jorja embracing Lorene, and thought to myself, *this is it*. This is what life is all about: Overcoming the impossible, enduring to the end, victory over self. Here was obedience, sacrifice and service, at the peak moment of trial. If anyone says there are no modern miracles or heroes today, I'll remember this moment. I will never forget the miracles and heroes I have met, among the rank and file of my ward.

CHAPTER 18

BAPTISM BOY

Saturday morning was heralded in by the beep-beeping of a workman's truck as it backed up our driveway to unload the wrong kind of drywall. Maybe it was experiences like this that made Edith Horvitz resort to particle board and a glue gun.

During the night, Gizmo had gnawed the soft pedal off the piano (just what every family needs—a giant, barking termite), Erica was crying about the burned pancakes she had just made (pancake trouble must run in the family), and Ryan was pouring dishwashing liquid into the automatic dishwasher (soon we'd have enough bubbles to entertain every Lawrence Welk fan who ever lived).

But despite it all, I couldn't resist singing and floating through the house. Today was Grayson's eighth birthday, and this afternoon he would be baptized. Nothing can mar a milestone like that.

I stood beside Brian, who was shaving, as I put on my makeup. "The great thing about permanents," I announced as I began to brush my hair, "is that they aren't."

Brian smiled. "It does seem to have settled down somewhat."

I gave him a glance and he quickly added, "Not that I didn't like how it was before . . . or ever will be again . . . or is right now," he said, trying to save himself.

"So are you ready for the big day?" I asked, letting him off the hook.

"Yep." He rinsed his face. "Have you seen Grayson?"

I laughed. I had gone in to wake him and wish him a happy birthday, but he was already up, sitting on his bed in his Sunday best, his hair slicked down with water. "He is so excited," I said.

"Well, he's definitely ready. He's been preparing for a long time."

"Zan said Nick would try to be here for it. Wouldn't that be terrific?" I brushed some blush across my cheeks.

"He's not selling Barcaloungers in the Azores this week?"

"I hope not. His own birthday is in two days, and I have the quilt wrapped and stashed in the trunk of the car, just in case he shows up at church and has to take off again."

Just then I heard some kids yelling out in the street. Then the front door slammed. I started down the stairs, and heard Ryan's voice. "Those stupid Chadwick kids," he was saying.

"Don't let them bother you, Grayson." Now Erica was speaking. "You don't need friends like that."

"Yeah, you always have us," Ryan said.

I followed the kids into the family room. "What's going on?"

"Oh, those dumb Chadwicks were teasing Grayson for being all dressed up," Erica said. "Then, when he told them he was getting baptized today, they said that's for babies and started calling him names." My heart ached for Grayson. The Chadwicks were the boys he longed to play with, the boys he had tried so hard to befriend.

I held him in my arms. "People sometimes say hurtful things when they don't understand the situation," I said. "Many churches baptize babies. Maybe they don't realize that you have to reach the age of accountability in our church."

Grayson shrugged, fighting back tears.

"You know," I said, smoothing his hair, "Ryan is right. Friends may come and go, but our family is forever. You'll always have us." Then I winked. "Small consolation, I realize . . ."

Grayson laughed and threw his arms around my neck.

"I know it hurts when kids are cruel," I whispered. "But the only thing to do is stand up for what's right, even if others tease you."

"Remember that family home evening lesson?" Ryan said. "It was just like this!"

I looked into Grayson's eyes. "That's right," I said. "Remember? Paul taught the Corinthians that we should rejoice when we're persecuted for righteousness' sake. It's hard to do, but just think of all the blessings you're piling up right now."

"Yeah," Erica joined in. "When we're all up in heaven, someone will say, 'Hey, what's that mountain over there?' and we'll say, 'Oh, that's Grayson's pile of blessings!'" Grayson laughed again, and Ryan patted his back.

"Maybe we should invite the Chadwick boys to the baptism," I suggested, "so they'll see what it is."

"Grayson," Erica said, "those guys should be happy for you. There's nothing wrong with getting baptized. You're *supposed* to!"

Grayson smiled, and looked at his sister. "We stick together in our family, don't we?"

"Just like Mommy and Uncle Nick. She'll always stick by him," Ryan said. "No matter what. Right, Mommy?"

Now it was my turn to cry. So that was why my children were comforting each other. I had never realized it before. "Right," I whispered. "I do love Uncle Nick. And I will always be there for him."

Ryan looked back at Grayson as if to say, "See? So we'll do the same." As they ran off to play, I felt grateful for all Nick's peculiarities. Without them, I might never have been able to teach my children unconditional love for your siblings. Now, more than ever, I was eager to see Nick at Grayson's baptism.

Soon Erica was painting a T-shirt, Ryan was entertaining himself with a collection of bottle caps, and Grayson had changed out of his church clothes and was playing in the yard.

"Can I play, too?" I asked.

Grayson grinned. Soon we were scooping tunnels in the sandbox, planting twig trees, rolling toy cars over a sand superhighway, and racing leaves across our pie tin lake. Someday, I thought to myself, this little nearly-baptized boy will be grown up. The sandcastle days will be over. If only I could stretch the day like a child's arms reaching up to his mother. If I could, I just might make it last forever.

That evening, my mother brought a beautiful bouquet to the baptism. "I remember when you were a little girl, and you'd ask me to arrange flowers with you," she said. "I often think of that, now—about you dancing in the garden with all the butterflies and flowers." Suddenly I saw myself years from now, handing Grayson a little shovel and pail for *his* little boy, and telling him how much I enjoyed playing in the sand with him when he was young.

"Goodness, I didn't mean to make you cry," Mom said.

"C'mere, Grandma," Ryan said, pulling her by the hand, "I want you to see my Primary classroom. One of my drawings is on the bulletin board."

Brian took Grayson to change into his white clothing. "Here—hold this, okay?" Grayson thrust a folded paper into my hand, and I tucked it into a pocket with Ryan's parking lot rocks. Moms, it seems, are what you have before you're old enough to have a locker or a wallet.

When we headed back to the font, the room was full of friends even though it was still early. Lara and Monica winked at me from the back row. My sisters, Paula and Natalie, had already arranged the refreshments, and Bishop Carlson and a counselor were there.

"Andy, this is my husband, Kirk." It was Claudia Lambert.

"I sure came home to a clean house," Kirk said, pumping my hand as if I were personally responsible. "I don't know what she's learning here, but I like it!"

How could I tell him that a burglar was actually the one responsible for Claudia's new homemaking skills?

"You should see my house," Claudia whispered as her

non-member husband began milling about. "Come over next week and I'll give you a tour. Remember the kitchen floor?" I smiled, remembering a floor so sticky that it nearly pulled your shoe off. "Well, that linoleum turned out to be bright yellow!"

I laughed. "Claudia, I can't believe you didn't even know what color your floor was—c'mon . . . "

"I didn't!" She was beaming. "After the *second* set of policemen came into my house and thought the place had been ransacked, I figured maybe I'd better get with it."

"Well, forty thousand cops can't be wrong, I guess . . ."

Claudia laughed. "And your counselor—Lara Westin— what a great gal. She showed me the best stuff to use on floors and walls. Andy, I never had a clue what to use before."

Good ol' Lara. No doubt they giggled the whole time, too.

Just then I felt someone take my arm. It was Jorja Willis. "We wanted to come and see your son's baptism," she said.

I glanced behind Jorja, where Lorene Hausman was standing. Then I gave Jorja a hug. "You are my hero," I whispered.

Near the door I saw Edith Horvitz and Rita walking in. Bishop Carlson was shaking hands with them. "Didn't recognize you two without your dance costumes," he said. Edith had brought along a crocheted cat, and was saying to it, "Don't piddle on the bishop, now." It was the first time I'd ever seen Rita Delaney snicker.

"Hey, look, it's Mr. Caldwell." Erica nudged me as Brian headed over to welcome our neighbors. They came! They weren't obligated and they came! This was something.

Then the missionaries walked in with a woman I hadn't seen before. I discovered it was Miss Galloway's sister, Jenn Strickland—the one who found my Book of Mormon. I shook her hand and began making introductions. There were so many people there that I didn't even see Grandma Taylor walk in and sit down.

"Mom!" Brian was staring behind me. I turned and

followed his glance to the back row where Grandma Taylor was proudly wearing the brightest turquoise bifocals you have ever seen. But even more shocking than her glasses was her companion: a husky Polynesian fellow fifteen years her junior.

"This is Kaulana Kealoha," she said, squeezing his arm.

Kaulana Kealoha? Brian was speechless. Of course he was thrilled that his mother had come to Grayson's baptism, but he was more than a little surprised to see her so ga ga over her new beau.

"Grandma Taylor!" Grayson yelled. The kids hugged her so hard they nearly knocked her over.

"I just *knew* you'd come!" Grayson was almost crying, he was so excited to see her.

"Erica, like my new glasses?" Grandma Taylor asked.

"They're really cool, Grandma." Erica snapped her gum.

"Kaulana has a black belt in karate," Grandma said. The kids all oohed and aahed, and began swarming around Kaulana, asking him questions.

Then Grandma stood up and Brian gave her a hug. "This means so much to us," he said.

She squeezed my hand. "I thought it would be a fun surprise."

"You certainly do know how to surprise us," Brian said, glancing rather obviously at Kaulana.

"Isn't he handsome?" Grandma Taylor had become a school girl again. "He's the neighbor I was telling you about. You should hear all the gossip about us!"

"All unfounded, I'm sure," Brian said, tongue in cheek.

Kaulana was every bit as charming a man as I would expect Grandma Taylor to choose, and it wasn't long before the two of them were staring at each other, all but ignoring the rest of us. "This is as bad as Nick and Zan," I whispered to Brian.

Just then we heard the roar of a motor, and the deafening beating of helicopter blades as they whirred above the church. It got so loud that one of the missionaries pushed a curtain aside and looked out the window.

"Boy, that's pretty close," he said.

"It's not the police again, is it?" Claudia asked, and everybody laughed.

"Hey, it's coming down!" Brian said. "Right in the parking lot!"

"What?" I dashed to the window. Sure enough, a huge brown helicopter was landing in the parking lot, it's propeller blowing the trees about and rattling the windows. Someone was sounding a warning through a bullhorn to stand clear.

"Must be an emergency landing," Bishop Carlson said, and ran out to see what was the matter.

Brian, the kids, and I watched from the window, as Bishop Carlson hunched over and ran below the blades.

Suddenly the motor died, the blades began to slow down, and the door opened. A sharp-looking man in a military uniform got out, put some luggage on the ground, then appeared to be shouting over the noise to introduce himself to Bishop Carlson. He then reached back into the helicopter to help his passengers out. "Nick!" Brian and I both gasped, and stared at each other in stunned silence as a second military man held the door for Nick.

"Oh, my heavens! The FBI's got him," Mother winced.

Zan stepped out next, and took Nick's arm. By this time the kids had bolted out to the parking lot, along with my mother, sisters, and everyone else. Brian and I stumbled behind them.

"Andy!" Nick said, sweeping me into one of his famous hugs. "I hope I'm not late."

"You're not late. You're right on time!" Grayson said, throwing his arms around Nick. "Will you take me for a ride after I get baptized?"

Nick laughed. "Maybe some other time, kiddo. I think the general has to get back to the base right now. Also, this is not really—"

"A legal place to land," Natalie said, her hands on her hips. "I'd like to know how you got clearance for *this*."

The general smiled. "Not to worry, ma'am," he said with a wink. "We have top clearance for *this* landing."

"I'll bet," Paula whispered.

"Are you sure you won't change your mind, sir?" the general asked Nick.

"No, I'm firm on this decision. I've enjoyed working with you, General."

"You'll be missed, Nick." They shook hands, then the general took a large envelope from the cockpit, smiled, and gave it to Nick. "A little something from the President, sir."

"Oh, this takes the cake," Natalie whispered. "He rented all this, even hired an actor, to try to impress us."

"And we're standing here like fools, listening," Paula said. "Let's go back inside." Paula and Natalie headed back into the church.

The general and Nick saluted each other, then we all backed away so the helicopter could lift off. As we watched it rise into the sky, our mouths still hanging open, a limousine pulled into the parking lot. The driver stepped out, and said, "Welcome back, sir," as he put the luggage in the trunk. "I'll be here when you need me, sir."

"Why don't you come in and join us?" Nick said. "Might do you some good, Robbins." The driver blushed, then shrugged and joined the crowd. Nick spotted Mom, gave her a big hug, then turned to the crowd and said, "I have two very exciting announcements to make, if you don't mind."

"He's probably selling partnerships in helicopter tours," Mom whispered to me.

"First of all," Nick said, "I have asked Zan Archer to be my wife and she has accepted."

A cheer rose from the crowd (and a gasp from Brian and me), then Nick and Zan kissed. She smiled the broadest, whitest smile I have ever seen.

"Ah, he did this to announce his engagement," Mom whispered, looking Zan up and down. "Well, Nick always did like to do things with style."

"You'll like Zan. She's great," I whispered to Mom.

"Second," Nick said, "I'm retiring from the Central Intelligence Agency."

Everyone laughed and started heading into the church again. "Nick, really," I said, snickering. "You are the biggest tease in the world. But congratulations on your engagement. Welcome to the family, Zan."

Brian hugged them both, and Mom kissed Zan on the cheek.

As the crowd thinned, leaving just Nick, Zan, Brian and me, Nick turned and said, "Andy, you are precisely right about my teasing. For years I have pretended to be a second-rate con artist, running one scam after another."

"What Nick has really been is a first-rate spy," Zan said.

"Oh, come on, you two." Brian started into the building, but I pulled him back.

"I know I've been obnoxious," Nick said. "I had to be, to keep my cover. I still can't talk about all the projects I've worked on, but—" he gestured to the limousine. "Let's just say that in all my travels, I learned some smart investing."

Brian's eyes grew round with amazement. "That's *yours?*"

Nick nodded. "And there's more. I know I've looked pretty shiftless, but I've been working my tail off."

"Nick, are you telling us the truth?" I couldn't believe my ears. "You've been working for the CIA?"

"He really has," Zan said. "I met the President this morning and saw him beg Nick not to resign."

Nick chuckled. "Guess who's the exaggerator in the family now?"

"Andy," Zan continued, "with all his investments, Nick's portfolio makes mine look like nickel and dime savings." (So that's why Nick gave such an amazing lecture that homemaking night.)

"Well," Nick said, blushing, "My work became my life. After college, the agency approached me about some special assignments that could use my abilities—"

"Like wheeling and dealing?" Brian asked, still skeptical.

Nick put his hand on Brian's arm. "Hey. Even a slick, fast-talker can use that ability to serve his country."

Suddenly I remembered his award-winning speech in high school, about serving America.

Nick went on. "In my case, I had to overplay it a little

so no one would ever think I was really on the level. The only way I could get ignored was to brag and tell outrageous stories."

"Here," Zan said, gesturing to the envelope, "See for yourself." Nick pulled a parchment letter from the envelope, and there, beneath glowing praise and gratitude, was the presidential seal and signature.

Brian, pale as the letter itself, turned to me. "Andy, I think Nick's telling us the truth."

"You never had an egg farm?" I asked Nick.

Nick threw his head back and laughed. "Andy, I haven't seen a farm in fifteen years." He grinned. "But I read a lot."

"And you never sold a diamond to the Queen of England? Or found buried treasure?"

Nick put his arm around me. "Don't tell me you've been *buying* those stories all this time. I thought you and the kids had me pegged as a fraud years ago."

Brian and I glanced at each other.

"I thought so," Nick said. "I'd hate to think I rented those rattle-trap cars for nothing." Nick had always shown up in a junky car, which had further convinced us that he was flying by the seat of his pants. "But you stood by me anyway," Nick said. "And that's why—"

Just then Grayson came out of the church and said, "Hey—doesn't anybody want to baptize me?" Brian, still stunned by Nick's revelation, snapped back into the moment at hand and rushed toward our eldest boy. "You bet I do!"

"C'mon," Nick said. "This baptism is the most important thing right now." Then he turned to me and chatted as we walked to the font room. "When I met Zan," he said, "it's as if I woke up. I knew it was finally time to quit this dangerous intelligence work and get married."

"Which could be even more dangerous," Brian teased. "No offense, Zan."

"Or Andy," I said, nudging Brian.

"I'd also been fasting and praying about it," Nick said. "I've been serving my country for a long time. Now I'm making myself more available to serve the Lord. I've talked with my bishop, and he thinks Zan and I might be able to serve a mission someday."

We stopped just outside the font room. "So why did you come and stay with us, if all this time you've had a limousine and who knows what else?"

Nick smiled. "You're my big sis," he said, sounding just as I remembered him years before. "And I knew you accepted me. Your family was my haven from a very bizarre, corrupt world. I'd walk in and the spirit in your home would be my oasis. I knew love was there. I knew the gospel was there. I needed *family*, Andy."

My eyes filled with tears.

"I also needed to try out my new covers. As soon as you guys were ready to throw me out, I knew the act was ready."

I laughed and slugged him in the arm. "Thanks for using us, pal."

Prelude music was playing and we all took our places on the front row. Bishop Carlson and his counselor gave wonderful talks. I glanced over at Nick and saw tears in his eyes. Brian's arm was around Grayson, and he gave him a squeeze. Then it was time. Brian led Grayson down into the waters of baptism, said the baptismal prayer, and then holding Grayson carefully, immersed him in the water. Grayson came up rubbing his eyes and grinning. Erica handed me a Kleenex.

After changing clothes, a jubilant Grayson was confirmed a member of the church. Ryan asked him how it felt. Grayson slung a fatherly arm around his little brother. "It feels great," he said.

Grandma Taylor hugged us all. She was actually too choked up to speak. Even Kaulana seemed touched by the spirit there.

Later, while we were enjoying the refreshments, I tried to convince my sisters that Nick really was a CIA agent, but they simply wouldn't believe me. "You've always been so gullible when it comes to Nick's stories," Paula said. "Here. Have a lemon bar." Brian and I looked at each other and shrugged.

Even Mom, though she seemed pleased with the idea of a classy daughter-in-law like Zan, just smiled sweetly when I told her Nick really was a secret agent. "And I'm Margaret Thatcher," she said. "You can be Imelda Marcos and have a whole new wardrobe of shoes."

I tried again at the little gathering we had that night at the house. "Mom, he has a limousine, and—"

She just shook her head. "You've always been the naive one, Andy. It will probably turn into a pumpkin at midnight."

So many kind friends came to the house to congratulate Grayson. The bishop gave him a journal, Brian and I gave him his first set of leather-bound scriptures, Erica gave him a handmade bookmark, and Ryan gave him a rock. "This is to go with the prayer rock. It's a scripture rock," he said.

As I looked around the room at all the people I loved, I realized that I was seeing a goal fulfilled. If the purpose of the Church—and the Relief Society—is to bring souls to Christ, then somehow we did something right. Here were four reactivated sisters (two by accident), ten non-members, and three relationships that resulted from efforts to reactivate.

I considered the last few months of Relief Society. We'd seen sixteen new sisters accept the assignment to visit teach, four had gone through the temple, and two had been baptized. Line upon line, we really were moving in the right direction. It was a very humbling realization.

Soon everyone had left but Nick and Zan. The kids listened in wide-eyed astonishment as Nick unfolded his real past. Then the family congregated in the kitchen as I drizzled chocolate sauce over some sundaes. Zan nudged Nick, "Tell them now," she whispered, beaming. I looked up. My heart would simply break if this whole thing was another of Nick's practical jokes.

Nick smiled. "I started to tell you this in the parking lot—"

"Not another denouncement!" Ryan burst out. His head was already swimming with the fabulous stories he could now weave for the amazed little faces in his kindergarten.

"Afraid so," Nick smiled. "For years you've been helping me keep my cover, even though you didn't know it. And no matter what I put you through, you always greeted me with open arms."

"Well, semi-open," Brian admitted.

Nick laughed. "To show my appreciation, I'm taking you all to Europe."

"WHAT?!" We looked like the windows on a ship—all our mouths fell open into a row of round circles. Not one of us could speak.

"Surprise! Isn't it wonderful?" Zan said, clapping her hands together. "We've already planned the itinerary— That is, if the university will give Brian a month off this summer."

"Are you kidding?" Brian said. "Professors have the greatest summer schedules in town!"

"Nick, can you really afford this?" I asked, after slumping light-headed into a chair.

"It sounds great, but we can't accept—" Brian began.

"Too late," Nick said. "It's already arranged. And anyway, what good is my money if I can't share it with the ones I love?"

"But—" I turned to Zan, then back to Nick. "You have a marriage coming up—"

"Which wouldn't exist if it weren't for you," Zan said.

"Let's face it," Nick said, dipping his finger into the chocolate sauce. "After putting up with me for all these years, you've earned it."

Zan laughed. "If only half the stories Nick's told me are true!"

"And," Nick added, "you'll break my heart if you don't accept."

"I am totally not believing this," Erica said, her eyes dancing.

I just kept staring at Nick, then all at once I lost it and began to cry. Brian held me in his arms. "Andy's wiring is crossed again. She always cries when she's happy."

Nick licked his spoon and winked. "Some things never change," he said.

"I'm so glad I'm marrying into this family," Zan said.

"Me, too," Ryan said. "I can't wait to tell the kids at school that I have an Aunt Shazam." Zan gave him a hug.

"Oh, I almost forgot," I said, wiping my eyes and hurrying out the door, "I have Nick's birthday present in the trunk. I know it's two days early—do you mind?"

"Have I ever?" Nick laughed.

Soon I was back with a giant bundle of wrapping paper and ribbon, which Nick tore off in characteristic style. "A quilt!" he said. "Zan, look. Andy, where did you get all these wonderful family pictures? Here's Grandpa Samuels . . . look at this one of me holding a string of trout! I can't believe you made this for me, Andy. This is incredible!"

"Happy Birthday," I said.

"Look at this one—my favorite photo!" Nick pointed to the center square. It was a close-up of Nick and me laughing, hugging cheek to cheek, the day *he* was baptized.

"That's my favorite, too," I said. "I must have had a dozen copies made, just to be sure I won't lose it."

After the kids were in bed, Brian and I looked through some of the travel brochures Nick and Zan had left. It was hard to believe we were really going to Europe. Soon we went to bed, and while visions of French sugar plums danced in Brian's head, I tossed and turned. I just couldn't wind down from the day's excitement.

Finally I got up and decided to clean off my desk. I gathered some bits of memorabilia from the last few weeks, to save in a scrapbook I kept in a closet. When I opened the door, I smiled. There was the pogo stick I'd carried to Claudia Lambert's house, and hanging beside it was a strait jacket in size 2T, from Edith's first home-making night.

I lifted down the scrapbook and turned its pages. Here I placed the printed program from "Chicks at Church," the family photos I'd used to make Nick's quilt, Grayson's baptism program, and a romantic card Brian had given me the month before to let me know that even a frazzled Relief Society president can still be enticing.

I went back to my desk where I had emptied my pockets earlier. There were the rocks Ryan had asked me to hold and the crumpled piece of paper Grayson had handed me at his baptism. I scooped the rocks into a small box and then, for some reason, instead of throwing Grayson's paper away, I unfolded it. In careful cursive he had written, "Dear Mom. On my last day of being playful, I want to play with you the whole day. I sure hope it's on a Saturday."

I smiled, then cried. Our family is forever, son. "Last day" will never come.

THE END